NOT A BLESSED THING!

A
SISTER MARY TERESA
MYSTERY
BY

Monica Quill

THE VANGUARD PRESS
New York

Copyright © 1981 by Monica Quill.
Published by Vanguard Press, Inc.,
424 Madison Avenue, New York, N.Y. 10017.
Published simultaneously in Canada by Beatty & Church
Toronto, Canada.

Library of Congress Cataloging in Publication Data

Not a blessed thing!
I. Title.
PS3563.A31166N6 1981   813'.54   81-868
ISBN 0-8149-0849-7   AACR2
Designer: Tom Torre Bevans
Manufactured in the United States of America.
1 2 3 4 5 6 7 8 9 0

NOT
A BLESSED
THING!

To
Catherine and Alex Cholis

One

Kim had promised Joyce she would keep Attila the nun out of the kitchen that afternoon, so she took Sister Mary Teresa into the sun porch of the old mansion on Walton Street where she could glare at television. They were still there when Richard showed up at the front door with the woman. Kim, sipping a martini from a coffee mug, her eyes closed after a truly hectic day spent running errands for Sister Mary Teresa, thought the doorbell was ringing in the program being televised.

"Someone's at the door," the old nun said.

Kim let that go by too; Sister Mary Teresa usually carried on a disgusted monologue with TV fare. It was only a delayed reaction to the sound of a cane thumping out of the room that snapped Kim out of it. Too late. By the time Kim got into the hallway, Sister Mary Teresa was opening the front door.

When Kim arrived at her side, she looked out the door to see Richard standing on the front porch, a woman beside him. He was just taking the woman by the arm, since she was turning away with the clear intention of making a swift retreat. The expression on her face said it all. Richard had obviously not prepared her to have the door opened by an old nun not much more than five feet tall, weighing close to two hundred pounds, and all gussied up in a traditional habit that had stopped traffic back in the bad old days. Sister Mary Teresa had hooked her cane over her arm in preparation for unlocking the screen door. That was when Richard saw Kim.

"Kim! How are you?" He was holding the woman by both arms now, from behind. He seemed to be forcing her to face the door, much as he was forcing himself to smile along with his phony cheerful greeting. "This is Kim," he told his prisoner. "My sister. The one I told you about."

"Your sister?"

Kim tried to get Sister Mary Teresa out of the doorway, but she had less success moving the old nun than Richard had keeping his charge on the doorstep. For a moment the scene seemed to sum them up: two people doing similarly unsuccessful things on opposite sides of the same door. Kim shook the thought away. It had been a bad day, but not that bad.

"Sister," she assured the woman. "As in sibling."

The woman's attitude changed from apprehension to curiosity as she peered at Kim. What she saw was a slim young woman with light red hair and the complexion that went with it, who wore a blazer and gray pleated skirt. Kim spoke to Richard and the woman over the starched headdress of Sister Mary Teresa that looked like a gull coming in for a landing after fighting offshore winds for several hours. It was, of course, immaculate, in every way as it should be. It had been designed by Blessed Abigail Keineswegs, their sainted foundress, her model the Hanseatic headwear of the upper middle class of her day. Kim herself had worn a modified version of it when she first got out of the novitiate, but soon afterward they had voted to dress like people, with the option of wearing the veil. The whole change in dress was optional, leaving Sister Mary Teresa Dempsey the right to go on dressing as she had been for half a century and more.

"His sister," Kim repeated through the screen door. "Same mother, same father, same ears."

"Good evening, Richard," Sister Mary Teresa said pleasantly enough.

"Hello S'ter." Richard's voice, no matter his height of well over six feet, his thirty-seven years of age, and his authority as one of Chicago's finest, was that of a kid on the playground thirty years before.

"And is this Mrs. Moriarity?" Sister Mary Teresa put the question with what was meant to be sweetness, but Kim could imagine the grimace of her smile, could almost hear the crackling of the starched frame around her face when she smiled.

"Could we come in?" There was urgency in Richard's voice and he glanced up and down Walton as he spoke. Kim reached around Sister Mary Teresa and unlocked the screen door.

Almost immediately the two nuns were pushed back against the wall as Richard and the woman came in. Richard propelled his charge before him and her expression changed from wariness to momentary panic. But then, almost immediately, she became docile. Richard's worried inspection of Walton Street might have explained her change in attitude. They all stopped when, from the kitchen, came Joyce's trilling voice.

"Who is it?" She sounded like door chimes.

Sister Emtee Dempsey—their irreverent semi-acronym for the old nun—not appreciating being pushed around in her own house, unhooked her cane from her arm and banged out to the kitchen, perhaps to see what culinary excesses Joyce was up to there. Kim led Richard and his charge down the hallway to the sun room. Richard pointed the woman to a chair, turned down the volume of the television, and went to a window where again he scanned the street.

"We should have come to the back door," he told the drapes.

"What is this place?" the woman asked, trying unsuccessfully to find the right tone in which to put the question. An elegant well-preserved forty, she stood in the middle of the room, hands on her hips. The full skirt of her olive green dress wrapped itself around her in a monumental way as she twisted to take in the room. Her hair was cut short and brushed forward, giving her a pixie look. She seemed torn between interest and fear. Her eyes went to a crucifix on the wall with some braided palm behind it. Emtee Dempsey spent the week after Palm Sunday weaving and plaiting the palms she brought back from church by the armful. They were stuck behind pictures all over the house; they adorned statues; they were everywhere.

"They make me miss my ukelele," Joyce had complained.

"Did you ever have one?"

"In case of flood we can make a boat like Thor Heyerdahl."

"The harbor is full of boats."

Kim wished Joyce were with them now to make some similar pointless remark that might calm the fears of the woman Richard had brought, apparently in the line of duty. He turned away from the window, slumped into a chair, picked up Kim's mug, and took a sip. His eyebrows shot up. He did not put the mug down.

"I'm Kim Moriarity," she said to the woman. "And I *am* Richard's sister."

"I'm Richard," he explained. "Kim, this is Cheryl Pitman. I want you to put her up for a few days."

Cheryl Pitman shook her head. "No way." She turned to Kim. "This is a convent, isn't it?"

Kim smiled tolerantly, at least she tried to. "We think of it as our home."

"That little nun . . . " Cheryl Pitman stopped, at a loss for words. She was not the first to despair of describing Sister Mary Teresa Dempsey, but the nun's outward appearance was the least of the difficulties. They did not call her Attila the nun because she was a pussy cat. She was old. She was a terror. She had joined the Order of Martha and Mary (known, inevitably, as the M. & M.s) at the age of eighteen. The Order of Martha and Mary had a Rule and she had vowed to live by the book. That is what she had been doing for sixty years and no amount of nonsense about renewal, Vatican II, or relevance would deflect her from her purpose, which was to come as close as possible, by her own efforts and the grace of God, to realizing the religious ideal set forth by Blessed Abigail Keineswegs.

She was the last of a breed. She had already been ancient when Kim Moriarity first encountered her at the college the Order had run in Glen Ellyn on an estate a tycoon with twitches of conscience had left the Order. With inflation, the exodus of many nuns into this world and the departure of others into the next, it had proved impossible to keep the college. Without the college, there was little reason to keep the estate. They had sold it for millions and then, in a gesture that drew praise from the *Sun Times* and *Daily News*, but not from the cardinal or from their motherhouse in Rome, distributed all but a fraction to the poor. In cash. Oh, it had been a lark, putting plump envelopes into all those outstretched hands. They kept the house on Walton Street and an endowment to maintain it. Of the half dozen nuns who had gone there, only three remained, Joyce and Kim and Sister Mary Teresa. Did it really make sense for them to hang onto the house?

"There are lovely nursing homes for aged nuns," Joyce had said to Kim.

"No."

"Kim, the Midwestern province is now us. Besides, you find her as difficult as I do."

"I know. But, Joyce, she joined for life. She's given her life. We are all the community she has left. It would be like abandoning her."

Kim had not added that it would be like abandoning one of her own major motives for joining the Order. She had had Emtee Dempsey for history in her freshman year. Thereafter, she took a course from her every semester but one until she graduated and went off to the convent in a corner of the campus to begin her novitiate in preparation for her first vows as a religious of the Order of Martha and Mary. One does not bcome a nun for a single reason, but Kim could never forget that Sister Mary Teresa had been a powerful one for her. She was the most brilliant woman Kim had ever met and she had yet to meet a more brilliant. It would infuriate Emtee Dempsey to hear it said, but she was one of the few adornments the Order had ever had and, as far as Kim was concerned, she could be as reactionary as she liked. Kim had resolved to move with the punches and look after the old nun as long as she lived. She was Richard's sister by blood; she was Emtee Dempsey's by vows.

And she had no difficulty at all understanding Cheryl Pitman's reaction.

"Can she stay?" Richard asked.

"Of course she can stay. Can you tell me why?"

Cheryl turned to Richard as if she too wondered how he would answer. The sound of an approaching cane distracted them. It was Sister Mary Teresa, of course. What was not of course was the tray she carried in her free hand. On it was a small chilled carafe and two glasses. She beckoned Kim with an imperious nod.

"Give our guests a drink, Sister. The drink is, according to Sister Joyce, a martini."

Kim poured, gave Cheryl hers, and then handed Richard the other. Emtee Dempsey, relieved of her burden, turned off the television set. Richard put his hand on Kim's arm and whispered, "We have to talk."

"Did you get your drinkie-poo?" Joyce asked, coming barefoot into the room, a flouncy apron tied over her jeans and sweatshirt. At sight of Cheryl, she stopped. It was obvious from her expression that she had not been told how many visitors there were or perhaps even that anyone other than Richard was in the house. Cheryl Pitman looked as chic and graceful seated as she had standing. At the sound of Joyce's voice, she turned, and her quizzical expression, the martini arrested halfway to her lips, the modish haircut, would have made any woman feel frumpy. The fact that Joyce *was* frumpy did not lessen the pain. She had meant her question for Richard and now looked as if she would give much to have back her idiotic words. Drinkie-poo, indeed. You had to know Joyce to realize there was irony in her employment of such a banality.

"Oh, hi," she said weakly to Cheryl.

"This is Joyce," Kim explained.

"Sister Joyce," Emtee Dempsey corrected. "We are nuns. Is your drink satisfactory, Mrs. Pitman?"

Like generations of girls before her, Cheryl Pitman obeyed the implicit instruction. She tried her drink and nodded in approval.

"Did you make them?"

"I did not. You have Sister Joyce to thank for it. Tell me, now. Why are you frightened of me? Have you never seen a nun in a habit before?"

"No. I mean, yes. But only from a distance. I've never actually talked . . . " She stopped, confused, and threw a helpless smile at Kim.

"It's all right," Kim assured her.

"What's for dinner?" Richard asked Joyce.

"Stuffed green peppers. You'll love them. Will your friend be staying too?"

"Do you have enough, Joyce?" Kim asked. "I'm sure Richard has dinner waiting for him at home. There is no reason for us to feed him."

"Kim!" Joyce cried. "What an awful thing to say. You're on duty, aren't you, Richard?"

"Joyce, if you don't feed me I'll starve. It's as simple as that."

Richard had put his hand on Kim's arm again. Before he guided her from the room, she picked up her mug. It was not yet empty. They went down the hallway to the living room, a monstrous place full of huge pieces of overstuffed furniture with lots of brocade, which is why they used the sun porch as their sitting room. Richard sat on an ottoman, sipped his drink, and repeated his request that Cheryl Pitman be allowed to stay.

"Doesn't she have a say about that? I really don't think she wants to stay here, Richard."

"She hasn't much choice and she knows it."

"Who is she, anyway?"

"Don't you recognize her?"

"Should I?"

"Ah, you otherworldly creatures."

Richard shook his head in feigned incredulity. Kim held her tongue. She was not often accused of otherworldliness nowadays and the fault, if it was a fault, seemed attractive. Her classes at Northwestern had swept her into an academic environment quite different from the campus on which she had earned her first degree. She did not think it necessary to call attention to the fact that she was a religious—the small silver cross pinned to collar or lapel was a weak signal—and for much of the day she felt like what she seemed, another young female graduate student, aiming at a career, hoping to make her mark in the world. But the world as a place where one pursued success was something she had put behind her when she took her vows. The truth was, she felt, that the world was too much with her. She needed the stern reminder of Sister Mary Teresa to that effect. But if lack of knowledge of the world meant not recognizing Cheryl Pitman, then Kim deserved Richard's left-handed compliment.

"That was Channel Eight on your set when we came in," he said. "That is Cheryl Pitman's channel."

"Does she do the news?"

Richard smiled wryly. "She owns it, Kim. Daddy gave her Channel Eight, Belmont Harbor, half the Gold Coast, and a regiment of enemies."

"Pitman?"

"That's her married name. She was, two weddings ago, Cheryl Stein."

"Aha."

"And her life is in danger. Literally. She has received a bona fide threat that she will not live to see tomorrow."

"From whom?"

"It would be a lot easier if we knew. I would like to dismiss it as a crank call, but she doesn't think so. Maybe she recognized the voice, but she won't admit it."

Kim said, "You have a suspect?"

"What matters at the moment is that she be in a safe place for the night."

"Three nuns don't provide much protection, Richard."

"Anyplace is safe if she isn't known to be there. Naturally I thought right way of you."

"That's nice."

It really had been easier, in the old habit, to tilt the chin and assume the manner that even people who should have known better expected of a nun. Did Richard really think she was without fear, that the prospect of having in the house a woman whose life had been threatened left her unbothered? Kim could imagine Joyce's shriek if she were told this. Sister Mary Teresa, on the other hand, would quite spontaneously behave as Richard expected Kim to. Kim had been mimicking Emtee Dempsey when she told Richard that, by all means, Cheryl Pitman must stay in the house.

"I called it sanctuary," he said. "That and a safe house. I didn't expect old Emtee to answer the doorbell. I should be used to her by now, but she still surprises me. It's like seeing a dinosaur in Lincoln Park."

"Can't someone like Cheryl Pitman afford private bodyguards? Why should she go to the police?"

"You got any more of this?" he asked, flourishing his glass.

"We're having wine with the meal."

Clearly he would have preferred another martini. He had had enough. Most of hers and one of his own. "Remember Uncle Henry," she told him.

"Did he have wine with his meals?"

"You know what I mean."

"Yeah. Yeah. He had meals with his wine. Including breakfast."

"Why did Cheryl Pitman appeal to you, Richard?"

"It's not unusual for people whose lives have been threatened to call the police."

"Even people who can afford to hire their own army?"

Richard frowned. "There's too much of that kind of hiring going on as it is."

"How do you mean?"

He hesitated, then seemed to decide to tell her. "I picked up a rumor that some goons were hired to do away with Mrs. Pitman. That was after her phone call."

It had been unnerving enough to think of Cheryl Pitman staying in the house, the target of an apparently anonymous threat, but now her own brother was putting them in further danger. If Cheryl Pitman was the target of paid killers, they might have followed her here. Kim remembered the nervous way Richard had looked up and down the street while Sister Mary Teresa spoke to him through the screen door.

"The house will be watched, Kim. In case. But I don't expect any trouble. We came here in a very discreet way."

Joyce announced dinner and they adjourned to the dining room, where Sister Mary Teresa bowed over her plate and got the silence she expected.

"Bless us, O Lord, and these Thy gifts which we are about to receive from Thy bounty, through Christ Our Lord."

Kim said Amen and so did Joyce. Richard added his in a voice that sounded as if he needed to clear his throat. Sister Mary Teresa kept her head bowed until Cheryl Pitman had said it too. She pronounced it Ah-men, not with the long A the others had used.

"Why do Protestants retain the Latin pronunciation?" Sister Mary Teresa asked, pulling her napkin from its ring, describing a modified veronica with it, and dropping it onto her lap. These opening questions of hers usually set the topic of mealtime conversation. Supper seminars, Joyce called them. Kim was more inclined to marvel at the old nun's seemingly endless store of lore and information. Such conversations would have been impressive enough if rehearsed, but they simply bubbled forth from a lifetime of experience and scholarship.

"I'm Jewish," Cheryl said. "Sort of."

"So was Jesus. Who are you hiding from?"

Cheryl glanced at Richard, then looked somewhat longer at Joyce and Kim. Then she shrugged. "Why not? Who needs a private life? Besides, you have a right to know. Someone wants to kill me. Really kill me. I don't know who it is, not for sure. All I am sure of is that someone wants me dead." She said this almost apologetically, as if she did not expect to be believed. Perhaps she found the thought of her own mortality impossible to grasp. "Look, it wasn't my idea to come here, you know."

"But we are glad you're here," said Sister Mary Teresa, and Kim found herself nodding in agreement. She only hoped her own expression looked more convincing than Joyce's. There was little doubt that Sister Mary Teresa at least meant what she said.

"I know she does," Joyce said later, in the kitchen. "What has she got to lose?"

Joyce and Kim were getting the dishes ready for the washer. Richard had left the house. Cheryl Pitman and Sister Mary Teresa were back on the sun porch, the blinds pulled, the television silent. They seemed to be getting on very well. Kim said as much to Joyce.

"She makes good first impressions."

Kim punched Joyce's arm. It was part of Joyce's persona, this constant barrage of down-putting remarks, but it was all therapeutic. By pretending to a negativity she did not really feel, Joyce kept it at bay, taming it against the times when it must really have tempted her. She had the toughest job in the house, Kim thought, the most menial. Joyce cooked and did laundry and dusted and cleaned. She did the shopping and oversaw the checkbook. And, in what she laughingly called her spare time, she typed away on Sister Mary Teresa's *opus magnum*.

By comparison, Kim's own existence seemed idyllic. Classes at Northwestern, out with people, pursuing her own studies, and doing research for Sister Mary Teresa at the Newberry or one of the university libraries. She was out there in the real world, which was the point of their living on Walton Street in the first place, but neither Emtee Dempsey, who did not care, nor Joyce, who did, lived much differently than they had in the days of closed convents, habits, excursions only by twos, and custody of the eyes.

Joyce lit a filter-tip defiantly, though she had taken the precaution of opening the back door for ventilation. Kim quickly shut and locked the door.

"Whatcha doing?" Joyce asked. "Do you want to get me in trouble?"

"Our guest, remember?"

Joyce took an enormous drag on her cigarette, as if courage could be inhaled along with the smoke. "How could I forget?"

"Doors locked, shades pulled. Those were Richard's instructions."

"And all that won't call attention to the house?"

"Let's get started on these dishes."

When they had the kitchen shipshape and went in to

join the others, it was pretty clear they weren't wanted. Sister Mary Teresa and Cheryl adjourned to the living room, leaving the television to Joyce. Kim went upstairs to her room to study. She found it difficult to get down to work, however. After she closed her door, she left the light unlit and went to the window. Walton was a street that was never really dark and never really deserted. Throughout the night people passed—in cars, on foot, the ceaseless traffic of the large city. There were bars and lounges and various less savory establishments in the neighborhood, and part of the nightly traffic consisted of their patrons. But some of the passersby were, Kim supposed, their neighbors. Why did the word seem almost ironic? Sister Mary Teresa might have said "I told you so," but she hadn't, not even when Kim asked her why she didn't.

"I give you credit for sufficient intelligence to recognize the obvious, Sister. Here we are, aswim in the sea of the people, relevant, renewed, and ... " She paused, then added with some relish, "ignored."

Maybe that counted as "I told you so," after all. But if Emtee Dempsey had been right that moving into the city and inhabiting the house on Walton would have no major impact on the neighborhood, she weakened her case by refusing to see any advantages at all in the changes that had occurred in the religious life. To hear her speak of it, everything had been just hunky-dory before. She offered up to God the suffering she endured because the life she had entered as a young woman was no longer the same. That was not her fault. She had no illusions about this new way of being a nun that, she was not reluctant to observe, seemed to be a way to stop being a nun altogether. On that subject, she was more than willing to speak on behalf of Blessed Abigail Keineswegs. Kim did not encourage this. Emtee Dempsey was intimidating enough by herself; she had no need to invoke the added authority of their long-dead foundress.

"Why shouldn't she?" Joyce asked. "Didn't they go to school together?"

Blessed Abigail had fallen asleep in the Lord several centuries before Sister Mary Teresa was born and even Joyce knew that much history.

From the window of her darkened room, Kim seemed to look out on a different scene than would ordinarily have met her eye. Richard had assured them that the house was under guard, ringed by protective policemen. It was silly to think she could see them out there, but Kim felt she sensed their presence. She also sensed another presence, a malevolent one, the one who wished Cheryl Pitman dead. Imagination? Of course. She was an intelligent woman. Nevertheless, she did her studying in a basket chair pulled into a corner of the room under a lamp whose light was scarcely sufficient to illumine the page she only fitfully read.

From below, the murmur of voices was audible, more so after Joyce turned off the television and came upstairs. What on earth would Cheryl Pitman find to talk about with Sister Mary Teresa? Kim closed her book and went downstairs.

"I'll make cocoa if anyone wants some," she said from the doorway of the living room.

"No, thank you, dear," Sister Mary Teresa said.

"Cheryl?"

"I'm fine." She lifted a hand that had hung over the arm of the chair she sat in. Ice cubes tinkled in the glass she held.

"Would you like that freshened?" Sister Mary Teresa sounded as though she were in the habit of plying guests with drinks. Had she found Joyce's hiding place for the liquor or had Joyce fixed another drink for Cheryl before going to her room?

"No, thanks. I can hardly keep my eyes open as it is."

"And I've been boring you." Sister Mary Teresa struggled to her feet. Her large rosary clicked as she did so.

"Sister, this has been the most fascinating evening I've spent in years. And thanks for showing me your arsenal."

It was then Kim noticed the Luger pistol on the table beside the chair in which Emtee Dempsey had sat. For heaven's sake. The pistol had been a gift from a member of the board of trustees of the college, a souvenir of World War II. That someone might associate such a lethal weapon with the formidable person of Sister Mary Teresa was perhaps understandable, but that the old nun should have accepted the gift was more surprising. Naturally she had soon turned herself into a bundle of information about firearms, she kept the pistol cleaned and loaded, but all her expertise was theoretical. She had never fired the weapon. It was a conversation piece and tonight, apparently, it had been brought out to show Cheryl Pitman how safe she was there on Walton Street.

"My dear woman, if tonight has been interesting, you must lead a dull life indeed. Good night and God bless you." And she left the room, thumping out with her cane, the Luger dangling from her free hand.

Cheryl had stood and now drained her glass.

Kim said, "I'll show you to your room."

Cheryl shook her head as she drank. When she took the glass away from her mouth, she said, "Don't bother. I know how to get there. Go ahead and have your cocoa."

"What on earth were you two talking about?"

Kim knew it was impertinent to ask, as well as condescending to Sister Mary Teresa. Kim least of all should have been surprised that a worldly woman like Cheryl Pitman would enjoy an evening's conversation with Sister Mary Teresa. Hadn't she done the same again and again herself? But then Kim was not a twice-married heiress who had been brought to the convent for asylum because her life was threatened. At the moment, as far as that threat was concerned, Cheryl Pitman seemed the essence of unconcern. She smiled at Kim.

"Bees."

"Bees!"

"Is that her field, or what?"

"Partly," Kim said, after a moment's hesitation.

It was a corner of a field in the region that was Sister Mary Teresa's scholarly interest. Her book concerned the monastic movement in southern France in the twelfth century. Monasteries might have been isolated, but monasticism was not an isolated phenomenon. It was Sister Mary Teresa's thesis that the monastery could only be understood in its wider social setting, that its wider social setting included an economic system, that the economic system was effectively agrarian, a consequence of which was that she must become an expert in medieval agriculture. Hence her knowledge of bees and honey. It was like her to concentrate on the vivid instance, something limited and seemingly peripheral, and give it the full treatment. If Cheryl stayed with them long enough, she would find the night's lecture on bees related to the monastery's role in the Crusades. Kim assured Cheryl that she herself had heard Sister Mary Teresa on the subject of bees.

"I did think it would be boring, talking to her." Cheryl Pitman's whisper turned into a yawn. "I thought I wouldn't be able to sleep tonight either." She touched Kim's arm.

"Good night, Cheryl."

Cheryl Pitman went upstairs and Kim went into the kitchen where, in semidarkness, she made cocoa. She did not want to turn on the light. It was two in the morning. She did not really want cocoa. How odd that she resented the fact that Sister Mary Teresa had devoted the evening to their surprising guest and had wowed her too. Kim remembered the expression on Cheryl Pitman's face when, standing on the porch with Richard, she had gotten her first glimpse of Emtee Dempsey. Maybe she was getting a little proprietary where Sister Mary Teresa was concerned, but there was another factor too. Kim would have welcomed the opportunity to get to know Cheryl better. After all, how many women whose lives have been threatened did she know? Had Emtee Dempsey sensed what Kim felt she did in Cheryl Pitman, an odd mixture of knowledgeability and naïveté?

Kim sipped her cocoa, half-seated on the little step ladder Joyce used to get at the high shelves, and thought about Cheryl Pitman.

It was three in the morning when Kim was lifted off her bed by a series of loud shattering sounds in the hallway.

She stumbled across the room, only half awake, and into the hall where she groped for and found the light switch. Joyce came screaming into the hallway. Richard was thundering up the stairs. At the head of the stairs, he stopped. Kim too had come to a halt. Equidistant between Richard and herself was the shattered, shredded door of Sister Mary Teresa's room. How long did they stand there, staring at one another and that door, thinking God knows what dreadful thoughts? Joyce stopped screaming and began to whimper. Richard started toward Kim, picking his way carefully among the shards and splinters of the door scattered about the hallway. At the door he lifted a foot, preparatory to smashing down what remained of it, when there was the sound of a doorknob turning.

It was the door of the guest room. It opened and it was not Cheryl Pitman but Sister Mary Teresa wearing a long flowing nightie who was framed in the doorway. A puffy nightcap pulled low over her forehead made the look she cast at Richard more menacing than the Luger in her hand.

"This is a cloister, sir!"

She spoke as if Richard were the problem, not the ripped-up door of her room, the room she had not been occupying. Richard took Emtee Dempsey's arm and tugged her into the hallway.

"You make a pretty inviting target, S'ter."

The shattered door of the other room then opened and Cheryl Pitman, rubbing sleep from her eyes, looked at the tableau in the hallway. "What's going on?"

Richard stared at her. "What are you doing in that room?" He turned to Kim. "You said she would be in the second room on the right."

"We switched."

"Without telling me?"

Sister Mary Teresa humphed. "Young man, what goes on on this floor has nothing to do with you. I suggest you go back downstairs."

Richard was clearly in no mood for nunnish loftiness. "We're all going downstairs. Pronto. C'mon. Let's go."

He took Sister Mary Teresa's pistol and more or less hustled her down the stairs. There were other men downstairs when Richard ushered them into the living room. The four women distributed themselves about on sofas and chairs. The men were from the police contingent that had been guarding the house. The volley of bullets whistling through the upper room had brought them out of hiding.

"No one was hit," Richard told them. He beckoned to him a man Kim knew to be Tim Farley. Richard and Tim had gone through the Police Academy together and were friends as well as colleagues. "Find out where those shots came from, Tim."

"I know where they came from. We could see the fire."

Farley had sent men to the building across Walton from which the shots had come. A newspaperman sidled into the house and Richard told Farley to take him the hell outside. When he turned his attention to the women in the living room he was all business.

"Okay. Someone just shot up your upstairs. You'll stay down here until we have secured the area. For all I know, there is still someone out there waiting to take another shot at Mrs. Pitman."

"Mrs. Pitman!" Joyce cried. "It was Sister Mary Teresa's room they shot into."

"And Mrs. Pitman was in that room."

"She insisted we switch." Cheryl reached out and patted the old nun's hand.

"Not that it did much good," Emtee Dempsey said, but it was clear she was touched by Cheryl's attitude.

"I wonder why not," Kim said. "Why would they shoot into Sister Mary Teresa's room?"

Richard said, "They wouldn't have known which room Mrs. Pitman was supposed to be in in any case. They must have spotted her through the window."

Sister Mary Teresa shook her head emphatically, making her great floppy nightcap bounce from side to side. "No one could have seen her go into my room. I entered first, with the light on, pulled the shade, turned off the light. The hall light was out when I left the room and Cheryl slipped in."

Richard had never liked riddles and Kim could see he did not like this one. How could Cheryl's attackers know precisely what room she was in and shoot only into that one?

"It's a wonder someone wasn't killed," Sister Mary Teresa said. She looked sharply at Richard. "Isn't it?"

"It's a wonder someone wasn't injured at least."

"Why?"

"Why! There must have been a dozen bullets tearing through that room, shredding the door, embedding themselves in the opposite wall. Any time you have that many bullets and that much glass and splinters flying around, it's a miracle someone isn't injured or killed."

"I think she means the shooting wasn't very accurate," Cheryl Pitman said in a small voice. She had listened wide-eyed while Richard gave his vivid description. Now he seemed to reverse his field.

"Or it was very accurate. As if they didn't intend to harm you."

"All those bullets and they meant no harm?" Joyce looked at Richard as if he were deranged. She was trying to recoup from her near hysterical reaction to the shooting, but she had no luck in hitting on some mordant tack to take.

"Perhaps it was meant only to frighten," Richard said to Cheryl Pitman.

"Then it worked. I'm not safe here. I want you to take me somewhere else."

It was Sister Mary Teresa's turn to pat Cheryl's hand. The frightened woman moved toward the old nun and Sister Mary Teresa put her arm about Cheryl and gave her a hug. They rocked together on the sofa for a moment.

"You're as safe here as the rest of us," she said.

"I'm endangering all of you by being here. If I go you'll be safe."

"You're staying right here," Sister Mary Teresa said, and Joyce and Kim joined in.

And that settled that, at least for the night, or what remained of it. It was nearly four-fifteen when Richard sent them up to their rooms. Cheryl went into the guest room this time and Joyce and Kim made certain that Sister Mary Teresa's room was habitable. Apart from glass from the shattered window and shades that looked like flags over Fort Sumter, the room was little the worse for having served as a firing range. Kim picked up the phone and tested it. All right. Sister Mary Teresa pulled the covers up to her chin, cast a baleful eye at the window, at Joyce, at Kim.

"Extraordinary," she said.

"Good night, Sister," Joyce said.

"Extraordinary in what way?" Kim asked.

"Knowing the right room."

Kim closed what was left of the door and tiptoed through debris to her own room. Sister Mary Teresa had made a gesture and it had not worked. She had put herself in harm's way and had failed to deceive those in pursuit of Cheryl Pitman. No doubt Emtee Dempsey was disappointed that all those bullets had not come whistling through the room when she was in it. How she would have gone on about that if it had happened. Not boastingly, you understand, but there was a lot of mileage to be had from the unctuous suggestion of the directing hand of God, the divine mercy, the concern of Him whose eye is on the sparrow, etc., etc., the implication being that God had kept Himself busy steering bullets away from her nightcapped head and diverting them harmlessly into the hallway. There wasn't much of an anecdote to be made of the fact that it was Cheryl Pitman who, after a little game of musical rooms, had lain abed while bullets screamed through her room. Apparently Cheryl had only been wakened by the reaction of the rest of them to the shooting.

Emtee Dempsey was surely right in regarding the assailant's aim as extraordinary. It could not have been a matter of luck. He had known what room Cheryl was in. No matter what precautions Sister Mary Teresa had taken, Cheryl must have been seen in that room. Either she had been visible during the big switch or she had unwittingly shown herself after Emtee Dempsey had gone into the guest room.

Kim realized, as she lay in bed thinking of these matters, that she was almost surprised that Cheryl Pitman's life really was in danger. It was clear to her now that she had not found Cheryl's story convincing before the volley of shots. There are still those who think Chicagoans find violence familiar and unsurprising. If that were true, Kim would have accepted the claim that Cheryl's life had been threatened as an everyday bit of information. But neither she nor 99 per cent of her fellow Chicagoans would react that way. Chicago is a pacific city. It is not without crime, but the average citizen is not assailed by instances of it. Kim found it incredible that there really were people intent on putting an end to Cheryl Pitman's life, people who would hound her down and kill her. Imagine someone deliberately killing a bird, a cat, a dog! How much more incredible when the target is a human person.

Quite apart from the mind-boggling nature of murder, there had been the further difficulty of seeing Cheryl Pitman as a menaced, endangered woman. She was wealthy; she wielded immense influence; she could command Kim's own brother as if a Chicago detective were under some special obligation to ensure her safety. Kim saw now that she had half consciously taken Cheryl's story of being threatened as the sort of fabrication a spoiled and wealthy woman might use to while away a boring afternoon.

Well, after that fusillade of bullets, there was no longer any doubt that Cheryl Pitman was indeed a target. Almost grudgingly, Kim admired the woman's courage, her ability to go to sleep in a strange house full of nuns who obviously made her nervous, to be jolted awake by an attempt to frighten her to death if not actually to kill her, and then go right back to bed again, in another room in the same house.

Sounds from downstairs caused her to raise her head from the pillow and strain to hear what they were. Had Richard returned? Was there *any* policeman in the house? With the irrational fear of childhood, Kim imagined that some crazed assassin had come sneaking up from the basement into the empty house. Soon he must start upstairs, one step, two step. . . . Memories of ghost stories, of listening to accounts of "The Hand in the Butter," were not welcome. The shiver of delight called for a group clustered close together, laughing away the fright of the narrative. Kim no longer felt the least bit sleepy.

She got out of bed and put on her robe. When she opened the door of her room, the sounds from downstairs continued. They seemed to be coming from the kitchen. Kim crept slowly downstairs, terrified, yet refusing to believe she could not freely move about in her own home. At the closed kitchen door, she listened for a moment, then pushed the door open. As she did so, she lifted one arm menacingly and gave an oriental shout.

"Where do you keep the coffee?" Richard looked at her over his shoulder, having turned from an open cupboard. He lifted his own arm and returned her greeting.

"In the coffee can."

"And where do you hide that?"

Kim crossed the kitchen and pulled the coffee from a

row of canisters in front of Richard. "You must be a big help to Peg in the kitchen."

"What are you doing up so early?" He relinquished the task of making coffee to Kim without protest.

"Investigating strange noises in the kitchen."

"Sure. Otherwise it's been quiet as a tomb here."

"You brought her here."

"Are you mad at me?"

"No." Kim turned to look him in the eye. "No. We're glad you brought her here. But what will you do with her now? Obviously it's no longer a secret that she's here."

"Do you know what I was thinking when I decided to bring her here? I should know better, but still it's what I thought. Disguise her as a nun. You know, one of the old habits. Everybody looks alike in one of those get-ups. It would have been perfect."

"If only we had known we could have gone on wearing them. How useful we would have been. Did we really all look alike?"

"Is the pope Polish?"

"Not all popes look alike."

"How many do we have at one time?"

"What about Cheryl, Richard?"

The coffee pot was on the fire and they sat at the kitchen table where Richard lit a cigarette, then frowned at it, as if it had not tasted as he expected.

"I've got to get her out of here. Maybe I should have done that last night, but I don't think so. Darkness favors both sides."

"Where to?"

Richard looked at her. "How about your place in Michigan? Emtee Dempsey suggested that."

Kim thought of their lakeshore house in Michigan, nearly two hours' drive away. Was it any safer than Walton Street?

"Richard, who is trying to kill her?"

He shook his head. "My job right now is keeping her alive. I'll think about the rest of it later."

The coffee was ready. Kim poured them each a cup and they sat once more at the kitchen table, looking down into the steamy surface of the coffee.

Kim said, "A religious habit isn't the only disguise."

"How do you mean?"

"You want to make Cheryl inconspicuous, but she would stand out in a crowd now, dressed as a nun."

"That's what I said."

"I have an idea."

He sipped his coffee. "You always do."

"Make it a uniform, not a habit. Dress her as a lady cop."

Two

The house on Walton Street had been designed by Frank Lloyd Wright and it may be the only private home he designed that has its own private chapel. The original owner of the house was married to a very devout woman, a convert to Catholicism who at those times when she could not go to church wanted, so to speak, the church to come to her. During her lifetime, Mass was celebrated in the private chapel two or three times a week, an assistant from the cathedral coming for that purpose. To Kim it all sounded very much like the English country house with its own chaplain, *Brideshead Revisited,* that sort of thing.

"Perfectly proper," Sister Mary Teresa replied to any criticism of the arrangement. "We religious have had our in-house chaplains as a matter of course: someone to say our Mass, shrive us, preach to us. Why shouldn't the laity have similar opportunities?"

"But only a few could afford it."

"The same could be said against convents; they could afford it, the houses of the laity could not."

"There aren't enough priests for each family to have its own," Kim persisted.

"There isn't enough of anything anymore—nuns, priests . . ."

Joyce interrupted, to forestall the jeremiad about the decline in vocations that was about to begin. "Well, there are certainly enough people."

Sister Mary Teresa smiled. She could not be baited by Joyce and this baited Joyce more than anything else. "There are exactly as many people as God wishes, neither more nor less."

Whatever the merits of that argument, it was a blessing for them to have the chapel. On the morning after the shooting, Sister Mary Teresa and Kim were in the chapel saying the Little Office, Matins and Lauds, when Joyce came in looking sheepish. She joined in and when they had finished and Sister Mary Teresa had sat, folded her arms, and closed her eyes, about to lower herself into her inner depths for the twenty-minute morning meditation that could not be disturbed by anything less than a 10 on the Richter scale, Joyce whispered in Kim's ear.

"Where is everybody?"

"They left."

"When?"

It had been just before six that they had made the big transfer. Dressed in the clothes Cheryl had worn the previous evening, Kim was led out to a waiting Black Maria, the colorful center of a bouquet of dark blue figures.

"You're under arrest," Cheryl called gaily after her. "It's like a dream."

The dream Cheryl Pitman was in was more like a nightmare. Yet when Kim went upstairs to wake her, Cheryl had had trouble putting sleep away. Finally she sat on the edge of the bed, rubbed the tip of her nose with the back of her hand, and asked if there had been any more shooting.

"I really believe you would have slept through it if there had been."

"Meaning there hasn't been."

Cheryl found her cigarettes and shook one from the package. Kim could not imagine why anyone would want to smoke at all, let alone at the crack of dawn. She marveled at Cheryl's aplomb. After last night, she woke to ask if there had been any further shooting and then calmly lit a cigarette. Did she think she was immortal?

"They're going to take you somewhere else, Cheryl."

"How I wish I were home in my own bed." Cheryl directed a thin stream of smoke at the ceiling. It might have been a prayer.

"We have a place in Michigan."

"Michigan!"

"It isn't fifty miles away. Sister Mary Teresa suggested it."

That seemed to remove all Cheryl's objections. She got to her feet and went like a sleepwalker to the bathroom, the borrowed nightgown trailing behind her. When she emerged some minutes later, Kim decided she was really awake. That was when she explained about the uniform.

"You're kidding." She peered at Kim with half-opened eyes and one side of her mouth lifted in an incredulous smile.

"I'll just put it here on the bed."

"I won't wear it."

"You have to. Cheryl, people are shooting at you."

"Is the uniform Sister Mary Teresa's idea too?"

There are little moments when character is reinforced or begins to collapse. Kim's impulse was to assert her ownership of the idea, to let Cheryl Pitman know that Emtee Dempsey was not the only one in the house capable of using her head. But it was more important that the plan be put into effect than that its origin be known. Cheryl took silence as an affirmative answer to her question. She nodded in reluctant agreement and disappeared into the bathroom with the uniform.

Downstairs, Richard was thanking Emtee Dempsey for the use of their house in Michigan.

"Her life is in danger."

"Her very expensive life," Richard mumbled.

It was the sort of thing they had often gone on about, Kim and Richard, the injustices of society and what could be done about them. Kim was proud to have a brother who was both a member of the Chicago police and concerned about changing what was wrong with their city and country.

"Sin is what's wrong with the world," Sister Mary Teresa would say. It was not her only contribution to such discussions, but you could count on that remark being made sooner or later.

"Okay, but past sins make present circumstances," Kim replied. "It's those that have to be changed."

Sister Mary Teresa conceded the point. She was not half the curmudgeon she seemed, or wanted to seem, Kim was not sure why. Certainly Cheryl Pitman's plight had gotten to her.

When Cheryl came downstairs in her police uniform, there was much playful badinage, but when the platoon of officers gathered on the front porch and Kim joined them for the flesh-tingling walk to the Black Maria, a sober silence fell.

"You're under arrest," Cheryl called, and her voice betrayed her own emotions. "It's like a dream."

The uniformed policemen with Kim in their center arrived at the Black Maria without incident. Richard and Cheryl sauntered to a marked police car and got in. Only after they were safely gone did Kim, wearing a veil, walk back to the house. It was that simple. Back in the house, she was given a big hug by Sister Mary Teresa.

"Brave girl."

And there were tears in the old nun's eyes.

After breakfast, it was business as usual. When Sister Mary Teresa prepared to settle down at her desk for the first of the two four-hour stints she put in every day, including Sunday, Kim went in to see if there were any research tasks for her.

"Yes, there is something I'd like you to do for me, Sister."

Kim sat down and opened a notebook, ready to take down titles, authors, topics on which Emtee Dempsey would want information from some library Kim could easily get to and Sister Mary Teresa could not.

"Mrs. Pitman has a daughter. Her name is Miriam. A lovely name. She is a student at a school not far distant from where our own used to be. It is called Birnam. The Birnam School. I do not know who Birnam was, or is. You might find out."

"You really want to know that?"

"I want you to go see the daughter. Talk to her."

"About what?"

"Just talk with her. Get her to talk. Listen."

"For what? What do you want to know?"

Her eyes left Kim, drifting toward the bookshelves that covered three walls of the room. "I don't know."

"Surely you don't want me to tell the child what went on here last night."

"Oh, she'll know about that."

"Not from me, she won't."

"Sister Kimberly." Whenever Emtee Dempsey spoke this name it gave her pain. At the time Kim joined the Order, the custom of taking a new name when entering religion was still in force. Few could have been more relieved than she when it was dropped. A whimsical superior had informed her that she would be known henceforth as Sister John Canty.

"The Prince and the Pauper?" she asked, astounded.

"Saint John Canty."

"But *John.* A man's name?"

Mother Superior frowned. For over thirty years she had been called Sister Mark Thomas. Kim was just out of her postulancy and deep in the unquestioning obedience of the stay in the novitiate. For perhaps four months she was Sister John until with relief she became Sister Kim, taking again the name she had brought with her to the convent.

"You were baptized Kimberly?" Sister Mary Teresa asked.

"Yes."

"Who was Saint Kimberly? One's baptismal name is the name of a saint."

"I don't think there is a Saint Kimberly."

"Then you must become the first."

She could have told Sister Mary Teresa that she had been baptized Kimberly Marie, but if she had, Emtee Dempsey would have started calling her Marie. She called her Sister, just Sister, only very rarely by her given name. Oh, for the space of a month or two she could not get enough of calling her Kimberly. That was when they had a paperboy of that name, towheaded, with glasses an inch thick, and a peering expression Sister Mary Teresa characterized enigmatically as an authentic Kimberly look. But he quit the job and for the most part Kim became just plain Sister again. The use of her name was reserved for those occasions when Kim had to be forcefully reminded of her position vis-à-vis Sister Mary Teresa. She was, after all, Kim's religious superior. So now, the morning after the shooting incident at Walton Street, she said,

"Sister Kimberly, it will be in the newspapers."

"The police aren't likely to announce it."

"There were reporters about last night. Will you go speak with Miriam Pitman?"

"If you wish."

It seemed well to put things on a formal basis. Kim was assigned to provide assistance to Sister Mary Teresa. The understanding was that this meant research assistance. It was stretching a point to make this include a visit to a private school for girls out beyond Glen Ellyn, but Kim was prepared, in the spirit of obedience, to undertake the task. Of course, she knew that the pose she was striking was meant to impress Sister Mary Teresa rather than the Good Lord. She would ask pardon for her teasing attitude that evening when she examined her conscience.

Joyce was talking to someone in a parlor when Kim went out. A young woman, hair worn long, with a lean and hungry look. And a pad and pencil. Kim had pulled away from the curb in the house VW Bug when it dawned on her that the girl had been a reporter and that Joyce was telling her everything she could remember about last night. So Miriam would definitely learn of the attack on her mother. But not before Kim spoke with her.

It was late April and driving out Roosevelt Road into the western suburbs was a breathtakingly beautiful experience. Because she had reason, Kim would have liked to resent Sister Mary Teresa's sending her off on this silly little errand, one that at most satisfied some passing whim of hers. When Kim had sat down beside her desk and flipped open her notebook she would have thought, if Sister Mary Teresa meant to ask her to do something connected with Cheryl Pitman and the incident of the night before, that she would ask her to go out to Union Pier, Michigan, and, using her connection with Richard, find out . . . find out what? That would have been neither more nor less of a wild-goose chase than her trek out to the Birnam School to see Miriam Pitman. Or so it seemed to Kim.

She had learned, as Richard had, too, that on occasion Sister Mary Teresa was capable of seeing something others did not see, not even one with the trained eye of a policeman. There had been the time, for instance, when it was Sister Mary Teresa's inspection of two pieces of metered mail that had revealed an embezzlement of astronomic proportions in welfare payments; there was a man in a cell in Joliet, to mention another instance, who would occupy it for many years because of a knowledge of Spanish that Sister Mary Teresa had surprised him into revealing at a crucial moment. Richard had been grateful for these and other surprises that had shortened his work, but he scoffed at any suggestion that what Sister Mary Teresa had done really broke the case.

"It doesn't work that way, Kim. Police work is a dull, tedious business, cumulative. That's why we have all these routines. Half the time they seem to be just ways of wasting time, but by and large, sooner or later, a picture emerges and . . ."

"No picture was emerging in the welfare fraud case, and you had no idea the mortician's assistant knew Spanish and thus . . ."

Richard was smiling at her. "Okay. Think it if you want to. Sister Mary Sherlock assists the stupid police."

"She did!"

"If she picked a winner in tomorrow's race, would that make her an expert on horses?"

"Beginner's luck?"

"You said it. Kim, it's not guesses that solve cases. But evidence that supports one guess among many."

"Speaking Spanish was evidence. So was the meter mark on those envelopes."

Kim stopped. Not only did she hate I-told-you-so's, her loyalties were divided. She did not want to champion Sister Mary Teresa against Richard, any more than she wanted to do the reverse. Besides, whatever he said, it seemed clear that Richard was perfectly well aware of Sister Mary Teresa's uncanny knack for seeing what others missed. It was no accident that he had thought of the house on Walton Street when he had to have a safe place, or what he thought would be a safe place, to put Cheryl Pitman for the night. Kim remembered the long conversation Sister Mary Teresa and Cheryl Pitman had had. Richard could not have arranged that, though it was the sort of thing he might have wanted to happen while Cheryl Pitman was in the house.

But Cheryl Pitman and the shooting up of one of their rooms seemed, as Kim drove into Glen Ellyn, a very different occurrence than the others she had just remembered. Those she had had an inkling about while they were going on. That April morning, driving through a world coming alive once more, an Easter world, Kim had not yet had that feeling and was accordingly prepared to mask her delight at being on this excursion with an insincere inner grumbling about Sister Mary Teresa's cavalier treatment of her. What on earth did she expect her to find out from Miriam? It was bad enough to be sent on an errand, but to be sent on an errand whose point and purpose you do not know is far worse. And if Sister Mary Teresa was being candid, she did not know the point of it herself. It all smacked of the worst features of obedience in the pre-Vatican II church.

Kim had to ask directions to find it, but at half-past nine she came down a country road and there was the drive into the Birnam School. She went on by. Like a dummy, she had not given any thought to what she was going to say when she asked to speak to Miriam Pitman. To speak the simple truth was to invite a swift denial. No school would permit a complete stranger to speak to one of its students without permission of the parents. Of course, Kim could not lie. How she wished that instead of speculating on Sister Mary Teresa's motives for wanting her to speak to Miriam she had asked her how she was supposed to go about doing it. She decided she would do so now. Let her figure out an honest way for Kim to interview Miriam Pitman. Kim couldn't even think of a convincing lie that would work.

At a crossroads filling station, she dialed the number of the house on Walton. When Joyce answered, the sound of the TV was an audible background.

"Don't let Attila catch you watching those soaps," Kim warned.

"She is in her study. Her brown study. She has closed the door behind her and wishes not to be disturbed."

"I have to talk with her."

"You want me to put her on the phone?"

"After you turn off the TV. Please. I'm in a booth."

"Lucky you. Just a minute."

Kim had far more than a minute to look out at the Illinois countryside from the miniature glass house of the phone booth. A young attendant came and held the oil stick up for her to see, mouthing the word, "Low." Kim told him to put in a quart. He cupped his ear. Kim opened the door and leaned out.

"Put in what it needs."

"What weight?"

"Thirty?"

He nodded, so it must have been right. At the same moment, Sister Mary Teresa spoke in her ear.

"Thirty what?"

"Weight. Oil. For the car."

"You're having trouble?"

"Not with the car. I've found the Birnam School."

"Are you calling from there?"

"I'm calling from a service station. It occurred to me when I came to the gates of the school that I had no legitimate reason for asking to speak with Miriam Pitman."

"Of course you do."

"I do?"

"Her mother wishes you to speak to her."

"Is that true?"

The half minute of silence was meant to be a rebuke. Sister Mary Teresa could scarcely be expected to be cheered by the suggestion that she was lying. When she spoke, it was dryly.

"I had an opportunity to have an extended discussion with Cheryl Pitman last night. In the course of it she said, not once, but many times, that she wished I could speak with her daughter. You are acting on my behalf in carrying out her wishes. If a child's mother wishes you to speak to her . . ."

"They won't just take my word for that."

"I shall call them."

"I can't imagine what you could say that . . ."

"Sister Kimberly." Twice in twenty-four hours!

"Please go to the Birnam School. I will call immediately. They will be expecting you."

So were the police.

When Kim had gone back along the country road to the gate of the school, she turned in and followed the long drive up a hill over the crest of which she had a most impressive first sight of the Birnam School, a brick building in the Colonial style, set upon well-landscaped terrain, not at its best in this in-between season, but undeniably impressive. The drive swung past the pillared porch and there were parking spaces immediately in front of the building, opposite the entrance. Kim swung into one and, having crossed to the doors and entered, stopped at a window just inside the door.

"I'm Kimberly Moriarity, and I would like to speak to one of your students."

The receptionist who looked up at Kim was middle-aged, with one of those apple-cheeked complexions that conferred youthfulness on her despite the gray hair. Her eyes crinkled nicely when she smiled.

"Miriam Pitman?" she said.

"Yes. Someone should have called you about my visit."

It was then that Kim realized that two people had taken up stations on either side of her, a pace or so back. One was male, the other female. Yang and Yin. The woman might have fooled her, but Yang had the undeniable look of a policeman. Kim could not have said what that is, but it is real and she had yet to be mistaken about it. Yang did not smile when Kim turned to him. His expression was that of a man registering what he saw for purposes of future description in a report. Yin stepped forward and took Kim's arm in such a way that it and her purse were pinned firmly, if painlessly, against her body.

"May I examine your purse, please," Yin said. She was pretty enough, in a nondescript way, but the heavy make-up suggested she had had skin problems as a teen-ager, which would not have been all that long ago.

"What on earth for?"

"Just routine," her companion said.

The receptionist was looking up at Kim with an expression of acute embarrassment on her pretty face. "They're from the police," she said.

"I guessed that." Kim said to the male cop, "It's because of Miriam Pitman."

"Let the officer examine your purse," Yang suggested.

"Go ahead. I left my rifle at home."

He was not amused. The receptionist started to giggle, then thought better of it. Kim took her purse from her shoulder and handed it to the female cop.

"Would you open it please?" Yin asked.

"Do-it-myself? Certainly." Kim made a gaping leather mouth of the purse and permitted Yin to peer inside. She put a hand in and rummaged about perfunctorily.

"Thank you."

"Why do you want to see Miriam Pitman?" the male cop asked.

The receptionist rose and her face was clouded. "That is enough! You've done what you asked to do, and that's the end of it. We are expecting Miss Moriarity." She said to Kim, "Go to the door on the left and come inside."

The two officers did not detain Kim. When she pulled open the door the receptionist had indicated, Kim thought, *Miss* Moriarity? What story had Sister Mary Teresa given them?

"Are you from a newspaper?" the receptionist asked. She had joined Kim in the hallway and they shook hands.

"No."

"You are a writer, aren't you?"

"What were you told was the purpose of my visit?"

"Dr. Dempsey said you were her research assistant and were gathering data about the Pitman family."

"Dr. Dempsey does the writing," Kim said, relieved that the technical truth had been told. No wonder she was being addressed as Miss Moriarity. Dr. Dempsey, indeed. The title was deserved, of course; Emtee Dempsey had half a dozen honorary doctorates as well as her earned one, but she never referred to herself as Doctor.

The receptionist put a Manila envelope into Kim's hand as they went down a corridor to the headmistress's office. The envelope looked like a PR thing. The receptionist bubbled away about the headmistress, Jane Corydon. Dr. Jane Corydon. The title was insisted on. It would be a doctorate in education, Kim supposed, and she was not particularly proud of the uncharitable thought. After all, Sister Mary Teresa had started the business of titles.

Jane Corydon was attractive in a career-girl sort of way. She looked up at Kim from a desk that was laden with work: correspondence, computer print-outs, several sheaves of yellow legal-sized pages. The headmistress's hair was pulled back tightly over her well-shaped head and her brows rose like accents above her glasses. Her interest in Kim was functional and that was all.

"I see you have been given our basic information packet. If you have any further questions I shall be happy to answer them."

"Thank you."

Had Dr. Dempsey promised a little puff for the school in the mythical work on the Pitman family she was composing? Kim would have to have another talk with the old nun about her extremely nuanced notions of truth-telling. It was a talk they had had several times before and one in which Kim had felt at the outset more than adequately armed with common sense, the moral consensus of mankind, and simple logic, but after an hour with Sister Mary Teresa nothing at all seemed simple.

"You must not interpret the maxim 'You should always tell the truth' as the duty to occupy yourself night and day with the utterance of true statements. You would shortly be carted off to a sanitarium if you did so. It is raining. My temperature is

98.5. The door of this room is exactly seven feet high. The number of concurrently true propositions is infinite. Therefore, not only would it be absurd for you to express them all, it is also impossible. No, what the maxim means is that, whenever you do speak, your words should be expressive of a truth. What that means is, of course, completely contextual. I am asked how I feel. Much depends on whether the question is put me by a physician in the course of an examination or by some vendor who has come to the convent door. In the case of the physician, my answer will vary enormously. If he is examining my eyes when he asks the question, I will not report on how my pedal extremities feel."

And so on and on. She made Kim's head spin. "Be ye wise as serpents and simple as doves," Kim quoted.

"Exactly," Sister Mary Teresa cried, a smile spreading across her face. You would have thought Kim had managed to find the scriptural verse that most appropriately summed up her view of the obligation to tell the truth. Perhaps she had.

Miriam Pitman was a slight fourteen-year-old with straight hair and wide watchful eyes that seemed never to blink. She hesitated at the door of the headmistress's office and then walked stiff-legged and rapidly to the desk where she stopped, the picture of a child doing something against her will.

"This is Miss Moriarity," Jane Corydon said, smiling toothily through the sentence as if she had managed against great odds to produce a person long admired from afar by Miriam Pitman. The girl turned and nodded in acknowledgment, and for the first time Kim became aware of the intensity of her eyes. As she had hesitated slightly at the door, so she hesitated now before putting out her hand. Kim shook it. "Miss Moriarity has been asked by your mother to talk with you. To interview you, really—mightn't we call it that, Miss Moriarity?"

Kim assured the smiling Jane Corydon that they could, indeed, call it an interview. Why not? Call it a market survey, call it taking a deposition. Kim felt like an impostor before this wide-eyed child and the headmistress whose smile seemed to have been frozen by a stroke.

"Where could we talk, Dr. Corydon?"

"Would you take Miss Moriarity to the parlor, Miriam?"

The girl bobbed in agreement. Dr. Corydon accompanied them into the outer office, asking if Kim would like coffee brought to her in the parlor.

"No, thank you."

"Very well." Dr. Corydon lifted a watch from off her ample bosom. "Would half an hour be sufficient? That is when the next class period begins. If that is not enough time, you may simply go on for another forty minutes."

Miriam Pitman went up the corridor a pace or two ahead of Kim, walking with the same ramrod stiff carriage that had characterized her entrance to Dr. Corydon's office. She opened the door of the parlor and stood aside for Kim to precede her. These studied good manners seemed meant as a tribute, almost ironic, to the Birnam School. When they were seated on opposite sides of a low table on which a bowl of lilacs stood, her large eyes came to rest on Kim's lapel.

"You wear a cross."

"Yes."

"Why?"

Tutored by Sister Mary Teresa, there were a thousand honest, if irrelevant, answers she could have given in response to that question, but she found herself unwilling, if not unable, to mislead this young girl whose wary eyes seemed to be recording a world she did not quite trust.

"I am a nun."

"You're kidding." It was her first natural remark. The corners of her mouth quivered in the beginning of an incredulous smile, she allowed her lids to veil her eyes, she put her head to one side.

"No. I'm called Sister Kimberly where I live."

"Does Corydon know that?"

Again there were dozens of circumlocutions available to her and again she avoided them all. "No. I'm here on slightly false pretenses, Miriam."

"I knew my mother didn't send you."

"How did you know?"

"She would have to remember where she put me first. I don't think she does."

The bitterness in her voice was unmistakable and Kim found herself sympathizing with it unquestioningly. After all, why should a girl be placed in a boarding school in what amounted to her home town? To get rid of her. To let someone else look after her. Someone who did such things for money. Dr. Jane Corydon. Miriam's speaking of her mother putting her someplace, as if she were an object, a misplaced object, seemed to sum up her position too well. In theory, Kim would pooh-pooh the thought that there are as many poor little rich girls as there are poor little poor girls, her skepticism directed at their parents rather than themselves, but it would have been impossible to sit in that school parlor with Miriam Pitman and not sense that she was more abandoned than the runny-nosed ill-fed child of a welfare mother who at least hugged her offspring to her bosom and gave it maternal love. Is that what Sister Mary Teresa had sent her to find out about the daughter of Cheryl Pitman?

"Your mother stayed with us last night, Miriam."

"She was in a convent?" Again the corners of her mouth started to form in a smile, but she brought them under control.

"It is a house in Chicago, on Walton Street. Designed by Frank Lloyd Wright. We live there, three of us, three nuns. That's where your mother spent last night. She was brought there in the hope that she would be safe with us."

"Who brought her?"

"The police."

Miriam seemed genuinely nonplused. The eyes continued to stare, but her mouth dropped open. Kim decided it would
be wise to tell her what had happened last night, at least enough
of it to elicit some sympathy for her mother, to break through
this arctic veneer of cynicism. Maybe Cheryl Pitman didn't de-
serve her daughter's concern and worry, but it was so unnatural
for a girl to feel this distant from her mother that Kim was willing to be the bearer of the bad news of the shooting to jolt
Miriam out of her protective disdain. And it worked. Kim's description of the bullets whistling through the house, shattering
window and door and slamming into the wall, was vivid, and
Miriam became a fourteen-year-old girl listening to an exciting
fearsome tale. Unashamedly, Kim dramatized the events of the
night before. Her mother's arrival with Richard. The policemen
posted around the neighborhood to guard the house. But it was
Sister Mary Teresa who captured Miriam's fancy, especially her
Luger. Miriam wanted to know all about the weapon, where it
was kept, who got to shoot it. She was disappointed when Kim
told her that none of them had ever shot the pistol. But she was
revived by Emtee Dempsey's effort to mislead snipers by
switching rooms with her mother.

"It didn't work?"

"No."

"But how could they have known?"

Kim shrugged. Let it go. Not knowing added to the
mysteriousness of the events. She ended with a description of the
way her mother had been gotten out of the house safely that
morning, playing down her own role.

"Where did she go?"

"We have a house in Union Pier, Michigan."

"She could have come here."

"Oh, Miriam, she couldn't. That would have endangered you and the other girls. She would never have done that."

It was difficult not to think of this wide-eyed girl as
vulnerable already, whatever her mother did. But the kind of at-

❋ 45 ❋

tack she was vulnerable to was more subtle than bullets. The presumed source of the attack on Cheryl Pitman would scarcely threaten the daughter too.

"Her husband," Sister Mary Teresa said, putting a corner of toast in her mouth. "He would share the money as her widower, which he would not as her divorced husband."

"She told you that?"

Sister Mary Teresa nodded. She applied marmalade carefully to her toast. The old nun had the odd habit of buttering and marmalading her toast a bite at a time, and Kim had never been able to decide whether this was extravagance or some strange economizing. Was Sister Mary Teresa really so blasé about a woman accusing her husband of plotting to kill her?

"He would do it indirectly, of course. Not that it makes a particle of difference legally or morally. He has hired people to kill her." She chewed toast judiciously, sipped her coffee, paused. "That is her story."

"Do you believe it?"

"I called it a story. There are truths in it, no doubt of that, but it is a product of her way of looking at things. She has been pampered and spoiled since she was a child. This distorts her view of the world, particularly of other people. You noticed how charming she is?"

"The two of you certainly got along well."

"She was dying to unburden herself, to put an interpretation on her sudden appearance at a convent for safety. Anyone could see that. I simply provided the required ear."

"She did a bit of listening herself, I'll bet."

"One primes the pump, yes."

"Has she told the police her suspicions of her husband?"

"That is scarcely necessary. He's an obvious suspect."

"You seem to be very skeptical of everything she says."

"Do I?"

"Well, you apparently doubt the story about her husband, and you question whether she really told the police what she told you."

"Yes, I suppose I do. But, as I said, there are many truths embedded in what she says."

"But what is truth and what is not?"

"That is the question, of course."

"Did you say anything to the police, Sister Mary Teresa?"

She looked at Kim over her glasses, a half slice of toast whose corner was heavy with butter and marmalade poised before her face. "I thought you might do that."

Tell Richard? Well, he already knew of the hired gunmen. Doubtless he would welcome a theory as to who had hired them. But then the snipers could lead him to their employer without benefit of anything Kim said to him. Besides, as Emtee Dempsey said, Cheryl's husband would already have occurred to the police as a possible source of her troubles.

"Murder begins at home," was one of Richard's less savory axioms, derived from his experience in police work. "If there is no friend to suspect, look into relatives, the closer the better."

"Richard, what an awful thing to say."

"It's an awful thing, I'll grant you that. But that's the way it is."

So Richard would have thought of Cheryl's husband if only because he accepted his own principles. Cynicism. His was a deserved cynicism. Miriam was far too young to distrust people. If she distrusted her own mother, what must her attitude toward others be?

If Cheryl's husband was the source of the shooting on Walton Street last night, then Miriam was in no danger. That a father should threaten his own daughter was too unnatural even for Richard's dim view of the species.

"He's not my father," Miriam said.

"Oh."

"My father's dead."

Dear God, what a blunder to chatter on like this and then forget the frequency with which Cheryl Pitman had gone to the altar, or however it was she entered into new marriages. She was exaggerating, of course. There had been only two. Her present husband had reason to fear being discarded and thereby separated from all the money Cheryl had brought to their union. In desperation, Kim looked out the parlor window as if suddenly overwhelmed by the sight of the grounds sloping away toward the country road.

"Birnam," Kim said. "Why is it called Birnam School?"

"*Macbeth.*"

"How do you mean?"

Miriam inhaled and sat a little straighter. "Robert Mackay, who was the principal benefactor of the school, got to give it a name. His wife had just died. She had been proud of her Scots ancestry as well as an avid reader of Shakespeare." Miriam recited this as if it were a set piece.

"Birnam wood," Kim said.

"The school was first called Birnam Wood School. But the wood had been made up of elms and they all had to come down, so they cut the wood out of the school's name as well."

And little Miriam's face distorted into a smile that was a perfect replica of Dr. Jane Corydon's. It seemed a note on which to end the conversation. They stood and for a moment looked across the lilacs at each other.

On her way out of the school, when she was passing the office of Jane Corydon, the door opened and the headmistress looked out. There was a startled look on her face, almost that of a child caught in some mischief. Perhaps it was because of this that Kim looked beyond Jane Corydon to the man seated in her office. Their gazes met for the moment or two before the headmistress stepped out and pulled her door shut.

"Did you have a good talk with Miriam?" Her voice sounded as if she were keeping it under control.

"Thank you very much."

"You have all the information about the school?"

Kim displayed her packet and, with that functioning as passport, continued out to her car. Strange woman, Jane Corydon. One might have thought she was ashamed of the man in her office.

Three

Sister Mary Teresa sat in her study at the cherrywood desk facing the one wall of the room that was not covered by bookshelves. Before her, neatly arranged, were the notes for the section of the chapter she was writing, in long hand, with a fountain pen, her extremely legible script the one achieved by what had been called the Palmer Method. She sat back to listen to Kim as for years she had listened to students. She hummed and nodded through Kim's narrative.

"And to think the girl's own father is dead," she murmured sadly, interrupting Kim.

"How did you know that?"

"His obituary was in the paper when he died."

"And you remembered it?"

"Certainly not."

"Katherine!"

Sister Mary Teresa smiled at her notes, then looked up at Kim. "Very good."

Katherine Senski had worked for the *Tribune* since the heyday of Colonel McCormick, and she and Sister Mary Teresa were thick as thieves. Mrs. Senski had been chairman of the board of trustees during the last years of their college, and the fact that she had presided over its dissolution created an even stronger bond between her and Sister Mary Teresa. Katherine was the kind of person whose pessimism was a form of cheerfulness. She might not, like her publishing mentor, think the redcoats were coming back, but she was equally capable of taking pleasure in the spectacle of the demise of the British Empire. It was the nature of things to pass away, and the better they are, the surer it is that their days are numbered. She had loved the college. She had fought for it tooth and nail throughout her term of office, devoting hours and days and weeks to the task of fund raising. To no avail. The college could not survive the dearth of students, the rising costs of everything. It had to be closed. On the fateful day, Katherine Senski cried, in public. Nonetheless, she had taken mordant satisfaction from the failure of the college. It fitted in with her view of life. It was the best endorsement she could imagine of the value of the school that it should fail. It was a feast of sorts to listen to her and Sister Mary Teresa trade, like versicle and response, negative estimates of the current course of affairs, the parlous condition of the country, the decay of morals, the banality of Church reforms, on and on, an endless litany of woe recited with such obvious relish that the two women came away from such sessions determined to live at least another decade to see their worst predictions fulfilled.

"What else did she tell you while I was out running all over the countryside? And under false pretenses, I might add."

One brow lifted quizzically. "Really? In what way did you deceive?"

"It was you who did the deceiving. Those people think you intend to write about their school."

"That is what I told them."

"But you won't!"

Emtee Dempsey's gaze grew cold. She reached before her on the desk and, though her eyes never left Kim, her hand fell inerrantly on a large piece of paper. She handed it to Kim without a word, allowing a reproachful expression to form on her face. Kim took the paper. On it Emtee had written the following: "Birnam School is located west of Chicago, is presided over by Dr. Jane Corydon, and is being visited this morning by Sister Kimberly Moriarity, O.M. & M, at my request."

"I have already written about the school," she said primly.

"You know this is not what they took you to mean."

"I am only responsible for meaning what I say and saying it in such a way that my meaning is clear."

There were times when Kim found it wisest not to reply. It would do neither of them any good for her to express her exasperation. Emtee Dempsey's dialectical skills were such that any objection Kim phrased, no matter how much it might commend itself to the common moral sense, would be so twisted, tangled, and refuted that she would be tempted to say something pointed, perhaps even cruel. And, of course, it helped to be able to tell herself that she did not want to provide Sister Mary Teresa with an occasion to engage in such truth-defying sleight of hand. Best to go back to where the conversation had left the high road for this thicket.

"What else did you learn from Katherine?"

"She wants you to stop by and pick it up. Apparently there is quite a lot."

"You wouldn't mind if I had lunch first, I hope."

"Oh, but I would."

"You would! It is nearly twelve o'clock."

"I know. Katherine expects you within the half hour. She wants to take you to lunch."

"Oh."

"She asked us both. Unfortunately, I have work to do."

"Poor you."

"Oh, but I enjoy it."

Was she really so impervious to irony? Sister Mary Teresa must realize that Kim had work of her own to do and that she was at her service as a research assistant, not as a messenger to be directed about the town on whatever whim happened to visit her.

But it was difficult to maintain the pose of one deflected from more attractive avenues. The truth was, Kim looked forward to having lunch with Katherine Senski and even more to seeing whatever information she had on the family of Cheryl Pitman. Before leaving the house Kim looked into the kitchen where Joyce was smoking a cigarette by the open door. She inhaled with closed eyes, drawing the smoke deep into her lungs. Then she let it out, fanning vigorously with one hand to direct the telltale fumes into the out-of-doors.

"Boo," Kim said.

In one motion Joyce jumped in surprise, opened the outside door a crack, and managed to dispose of the cigarette. When she saw who it was, she made a face and went out on the porch to retrieve her cigarette.

"These things cost money."

"So do doctors."

"Please, no moralizing. God understands. You don't have to spend the day here with Emtee Dempsey groaning away in her study. What is she on, the Black Plague?"

"What did you tell the reporter?"

Joyce brought the filter-tip to her lips, squinted at Kim through a smarting swirl of smoke, and smiled in what was meant to be a world-weary way. "They'll spell your name right, don't worry."

"And yours too, I'll bet."

"They *were* rather curious about my reactions under fire."

"You screamed a lot."

"A diversionary tactic. It worked. They stopped shooting."

"They."

"It?"

"I won't be having lunch here."

"Of course you will. It's ready now. I was just going to call you in."

"I'm being taken to lunch by Katherine Senski."

"Have her come here. She loves my cooking."

"So do I. We all do. I'm on assignment."

Joyce went to the sink, ran water, held her cigarette under it. It went out with a fizzle and she put it in the garbage. Kim had been meaning to tell her that this method of extinguishing her cigarette created a most offensive clue to the fact that she had been smoking. But the moment did not seem propitious. Joyce did not welcome any remark that seemed to criticize her smoking, and Kim did not blame her. Whatever relief tobacco offered her, she richly deserved. Besides, it provided her with the heroic task of quitting, or trying to quit, during Advent and Lent.

"Kim, you really ought to draw the line with her. She's turned you into an errand girl. A gopher. Go for this, go for that. You're too intelligent to be used like that."

"You cook."

Joyce made a face. "Ugh. I know. It's the only effective way I know to diet."

"That's what I think of running errands."

"Oh, go and have lunch somewhere."

"Peace."

"And carrots."

"Shame on you."

"And also on you."

Sometimes Kim thought Joyce was the most traditional nun of the three of them. She performed her menial tasks as housekeeper, she kept fresh flowers on the altar in their little chapel, and she had in a corner of the kitchen a statue of the Sacred Heart before which a vigil light burned continually. She recited fifteen decades of the rosary every day and sent away to church goods houses for the supplies of holy cards she dished out to salesmen who came to the door and to kids in the neighborhood. She included them in her letters too. So what if she wore denim wrap-around skirts and polka-dot blouses and sneaked a pack and a half of cigarettes a day? Joyce belonged to a type that has inhabited convents for centuries. Beside her, Sister Mary Teresa and Kim were hardly recognizable as nuns. Sister Mary Teresa, at her desk day in and day out, adding page after page to the scholarly magnum opus that was one large part of her reason for living, was an untypical nun, whether of the old style or the new. Insofar as Kim was anything, she was meant, she supposed, to become a pale carbon of Sister Mary Teresa, though for what purpose was somewhat unclear. The Order of Martha and Mary no longer had an institution of higher learning in which to put to practical effect the doctorate she was working for, and if she simply put herself on the academic job market eventually—where, given the present climate, she should do quite well, colleges and universities being under the pressure they were to add women to their faculties—how would she differ from a bachelor girl pursuing a career for the intrinsic pleasure to be had from doing well what one has been trained to do? That had not been Kim's purpose for entering the Order; that was not her goal when she had taken vows of poverty, chastity, and obedience. Yet what were the alternatives? She shut out this line of thought. She sounded like Sister Mary Teresa at her worst. But then, that was as good a preparation as any for lunch with Katherine Senski.

Kim put the Bug in a parking garage a block from the *Trib* tower and was really not surprised to find Katherine Senski pacing back and forth in front of the building. She wore a navy blue silk dress that fell in tiers from the round white collar: a capelike portion that fell to her elbows, a sort of miniskirt section that feel to midthigh, and the main skirt that fell to midcalf. All three sections were at the moment whipping like pennants in the brisk breeze off the lake. She had one hand pressed firmly on the crown of the wide-brimmed straw hat and, as soon as she recognized Kim, raised it to flag down a taxi. As a result, her hat lifted in the breeze and went like an errant Frisbie down the street. Kim went off after it, and managed to catch it in mid-air. There was actually applause as she turned to bring it back to Katherine Senski. What a great little retriever I am, she thought, and in every sense of the term. Katherine Senski now stood with her hand clamped to the top of her head, as if she thought the thick braided hair wound round her head might also go sailing off on a puff of lake breeze. A taxi came to a stop at the curb.

"I just parked my car," Kim said, handing her the hat. "I could have driven."

"You would find no place to park."

Into the cab they got, Katherine told the driver Berghof's, put her hat on her lap, turned and smiled at Kim.

"You look marvelous."

"So do you."

"I do not. I look old. I am old. What a marvelous thing youth is. Old ladies told me that when I was young, and I thought them as dotty as you think me. How is Emtee Dempsey?"

"Hard at work."

A snorting laugh. "Of that I am sure. She is the most remarkable woman I have ever known."

"That is a large statement."

"I know. It is also true. And just plain true, not true in the Emtee or Pickwickian sense. If there were justice in the world, she would be president."

Did Katherine think she would ingratiate herself with her by praising Sister Mary Teresa? But that was silly. Katherine Senski had no need to curry favor with Kim, and Kim did not need to be told of Sister Mary Teresa's accomplishments. What

Katherine did not know was that it could be a difficult thing to live with someone like her heroine on a day-to-day basis. For that matter, Katherine was some kind of woman herself.

When they were seated at Berghof's and Katherine had ordered beer for the two of them, Kim told her about the events of the previous night. But Katherine had already heard it from Sister Mary Teresa and she had also seen the story the *Trib* would be running.

"Sister Mary Teresa wanted to know about the family."

"Yes."

Katherine produced a Manila envelope that looked very full, and it was, of clippings. "Quite a lot? No. That's what's fit to print. What is there only between the lines is that Cheryl's family has had a stormy time of it back through at least three generations. Her great-grandfather, Simon Schatz, pushed a cart through the streets of Chicago. He arrived in the city with a dollar in his pocket and he died in a bed in his mansion on the Gold Coast. The transition took him over forty years. From junkman to yachtsman in a matter of decades. The real mystery surrounding his last days had to do with the yacht." She paused to sip her beer.

"It sank?"

"That was probably the intention. No, it was the fact that it floated that created the mystery."

"A yacht that floats is a mystery?" How like Sister Mary Teresa she was.

"When there are three dead bodies aboard, yes."

"Good Lord."

"The dead were Simon's wife of over fifty years, his son, and his daughter-in-law. They had set out for Mackinac with two teen-aged boys as crew. A storm blew up and they were given up for lost. But weeks later the boat drifted into sight off Chicago. The two boys were gone, presumably swept overboard in the storm, though their bodies were never found."

"What did the others die of?"

"Food poisoning."

"And Simon was left alone?"

"He had a daughter and she lived at home, a widow with a son. Her married name was Stein. The son was Cheryl's father. There was talk about the cause of the death of those on board the yacht. The name of which, by the way, was *The Albatross.* I can remember the speculation when I was a girl. It was thought that Simon had wished to clear the way for his daughter to be his sole heir. Or she had."

"Why on earth would he want to kill his own son?"

"Because of the girl he had married. She was Irish, she had worked as a maid in several houses in what was now Simon's neighborhood. The old man did not like attention drawn to his own humble origins, and he felt no affinity at all with his daughter-in-law. That she was childless seemed a divine judgment on the marriage. He did not even pretend to be happy that such a woman would come into control of some portion of the fortune he had amassed."

"But his wife!"

"She was old, she was ill, her death could hardly be regarded as an unmitigated evil."

"I don't think I would have liked Simon."

"On the contrary, he would have charmed you out of your shoes. He lived on and on. Even at eighty, he dominated a room, not because he was rich, not because he was powerful, but because of his personality. He had no illusions left and he saw things with a cold but understanding eye. And he was very witty."

"What was his grandson's name?"

"John. He died horribly on the El before Cheryl married. For the first time. Witnesses said he was pushed. Death was swift. He landed on the third rail."

"Pushed by whom?"

"The problem was not to find an enemy, but to select from the host of his enemies the one responsible. No descriptions gathered from the other passengers led the police to an arrest. Dozens of people were questioned. They formed lines in the hallways of police headquarters. There was a festive air about the place. I was a young reporter then. It was gay as an Irish wake. I remember thinking that not even the police wanted to catch and accuse and prosecute the person who had rid the city of John Stein."

"Why? What sort of person was he?"

The waiter came and Katherine Senski ordered more beer, but they selected their lunch too. As always at noon, Berghof's was crowded, the waiters hurried, the diners youthful and exuberant.

"John Stein was worthless. What was once called a ne'er-do-well. And he was a snob. Old Simon turned into a snob when he became wealthy, but it was forgivable in him. For one thing, he had earned it; for another, however much he tried to forget it, everyone else knew he had once pushed that cart through the streets. But John Stein had done nothing. He had been born into wealth and ease, he had been an awful student, and he had no business sense whatever. Moreover, he was stingy. It was said of him that the only good thing he ever produced was Cheryl. His widow became the sole heir of the Schatz fortune, which went on increasing and multiplying in the fertile air of bank vaults. The money Cheryl came into at her twenty-first birthday made an astronomical sum. The family, in short, has had a checkered history."

"Last night's shooting fits right into the picture, doesn't it?"

Their Wiener schnitzel arrived and Katherine Senski addressed herself to it with undivided attention. Images of the Cheryl Pitman who had spent last night on Walton Street distracted Kim. Her marriages seemed a peccadillo compared to the misbehavior and misfortune of her forebears. What tragedy Simon had shored up when he accumulated his fortune, pushing his cart out of the streets of poverty onto Lake Shore Drive! To what end? Had it made him happy? Whether or not he was responsible for his wife's death and those of his son and daughter-in-law, the accusation pointed to the negative effects of wealth. It was the same money that had made his grandson obnoxious and had made Cheryl doubt that either of her husbands loved her for herself and not the enormous sum of money that grew more enormous day by day, month by month, year by year.

"It makes me glad to remember the way we just gave away the money we received from the sale of the school."

"Grandstanding," Katherine Senski snorted. "No lasting benefit was achieved. It would have made more sense to invest it and bequeath the interest to the poor."

"We thought of that."

"I know you did."

"Then you must know why we rejected the idea."

"I know the reason. I thought it silly. And I was not alone."

Indeed, she had not been alone. Sister Mary Teresa regarded the argument that creating a foundation would call for administrators who would draw off a significant percentage of the earnings in salary and thus simply add to the class of drones living off usurious interest as theologically unsound and, worse, insincere. "Would you do it if no one knew?" was the question Sister Mary Teresa put to the assemblage of her sisters in religion and she humphed in skepticism when it was held they must give public witness to their beliefs. But hanging onto the money was conspicuous too, and it did not seem to go with their vow of poverty that they should have investments in seven figures. Kim had stopped having this argument with Sister Mary Teresa when the old nun pointed out that the three of them on Walton Street were sustained by an endowment that removed all need for worry from their lives. Even so, Kim continued to think Cheryl and her family would have been better off without their wealth.

"She's wrong to think Amos Pitman hired someone to shoot at her," Katherine Senski said.

"Are there other people with reasons to want her dead?"

"There may be people who want her dead, but Amos is not among them. He certainly would not be stupid enough to finance any attempt on her life."

"Why not?"

"Because he would be the first one suspected of it."

"Who would be next?"

Katherine's hand went to her dangling earrings; her eyelids went to half-mast; she considered the question. "Herbert."

"The brother?"

"Oh, yes. You will find among the clippings I gave you reviews of a biography of their father. Cheryl commissioned this book over Herbert's violent objections. She knew from the outset the kind of book she wanted, and she could afford to buy an author willing to write it. To call it a eulogy would be understatement. Herbert was furious. He got himself asked onto various talk shows and he talked, about his father, about that book. Piety is not his long suit, but then, Cheryl has enough for both of them. She tried to sue him for libel and was dissuaded from it. She and her husband managed to gain some kind of control over his trust fund."

"Because he criticized a biography of his father?"

"Because he showed irresponsibility in the handling of money. He was just handing out fistfuls of cash to people."

"Shame on him."

"You can see the risk the M & M s were running when they did the same thing."

"Is there a law against charity?"

"Actually, the IRS did get involved. They don't relish the idea of sums of money changing hands without getting taxed."

"I think I like Herbert."

"Well, Cheryl doesn't. Now they are involved in yet

another dispute. Among the things Herbert inherited, and that was not included in the funds Cheryl and Amos Pitman managed to tie up, is the mansion on the North Shore, Simon's house. Herbert has been offered a large sum for it. The buyer wants to raze it and put up a high-rise. Cheryl heads a committee formed to get the house declared an historic monument. So the lines are drawn again."

"Why would Cheryl suspect her husband when she has this sort of struggle going on with her brother?"

Katherine smiled. "Perhaps she takes it no more seriously than anyone else. They are like two children squabbling in a nursery. And then there is his store." Katherine looked sharply at Kim. "*Does* Cheryl Pitman suspect her husband?"

Kim grew wary. All she had was hearsay. The fact that her source was Emtee Dempsey only made her more wary. She said she supposed Cheryl and Herbert never saw each other.

"On the contrary. They meet regularly, if only to argue. She is a customer at his store. Once he called the police to have her removed from the premises. One such episode would suffice to estrange most people, but neither Cheryl nor Herbert seems willing to believe their disagreement is real; the other has to give in sooner or later."

"Can men be hired in this town to shoot at people?"

"I suppose."

"Where?"

"Are you in the market?"

"Not if you answer my question."

"I have no idea."

"Katherine, you know everything."

"It's sweet of you to say so, Sister, but I am not omniscient. You have me confused with someone else. Who mentioned hired gunmen, your brother?"

"Yes."

"And he brought Cheryl Pitman to Walton Street? Very nice."

"Richard thought she would be safe with us."

"How wrong he was. Where is she now?"

"I wasn't told." This was a technical, Emtee Dempsey truth and Kim avoided Katherine's eyes.

"I would bet Sister Mary Teresa knows."

"So would I."

It was Peg, Richard's' wife, whom Kim saw next, her harried sister-in-law who could not quite bring herself to look to Kim for sympathy. Richard was upstairs, asleep. He had come home exhausted and gone right to bed, although it was noon and Peg was up to her ears in laundry and kids and was a nervous wreck from worrying about Richard's assignment to provide security for Cheryl Pitman.

"I know I'm supposed to take his work in stride, but that woman's trouble, Kim, I just know it. She could hire an army to look after her if she were really worried. Why does she have to go to the police? With all the things going on in this city they assign a dozen people to look after her. Imagine."

"Where is a cop when you need one?"

"Exactly." But Peg managed a smile. "And what a treat for you to put her up on Walton Street. Did they really shoot up the place?"

"Has it been on the news?"

"I don't know." Meaning that Richard had told her. Kim was almost surprised, knowing Peg's excitability, but then she had a right to know. Whatever danger threatened Cheryl Pitman, it did not stem from Peg. "Is instant all right?"

"Of course."

Kim's nephew Billy sat on the kitchen floor, eighteen months of fat and good humor, happily banging pans and pots he had dragged from the cupboards. A toy box in the next room overflowed with expensive toys, among them the educational ones Kim had given Billy, but he preferred the contents of the cupboards, perhaps because they made more noise. Sarah and

Edward sat before the TV in little chairs, avidly listening to Kermit the Frog. Peg, despite her somewhat frenetic manner, handled the house and her three children with an aplomb Kim marveled at more after every occasion that she sat with the kids while Peg and Richard went out. After only a few hours bedtime seemed a reprieve and, much as she liked kids, Kim could not imagine spending day after day with them, cooking and all the rest. She did not admire the sense she had of escaping when Richard and Peg returned and she could go back to the peace and quiet of Walton Street.

"Sometimes I wonder if I became a nun out of selfishness. We do lead undemanding lives."

"I don't," Sister Mary Teresa said. "And neither do you. It is a matter of calling. Married people see our life as impossibly burdensome. And so it would be if one did not have a vocation. 'Each has his gift from the Lord.' "

It seemed too easy a justification of their unworried lives. Not that they didn't keep busy and work hard. God knows, Sister Mary Teresa was as industrious as any scholar Kim had ever known, pulled up to her desk, immobile by the hour, pressing forward with her book. And Joyce. How many housewives were as tied to their houses as Joyce was to theirs? And, untypical as this day was, Kim herself did not have to cede to anyone. A terrified sleepless night, up at dawn, a long drive into the suburbs to interview Miriam, home again, home again, jiggedy jog, only to fly off to lunch with Katherine Senski and pick up an envelope of clippings that might or might not be pertinent to anything but were certain to appeal to Sister Mary Teresa's curiosity. Swinging past Richard's on her way back to Walton Street now seemed an uninspired idea, with him asleep and Peg obviously in no mood or condition to entertain sisters-in-law. She had some on the other side as well. The truth was that Kim had come away from Katherine Senski's long narrative about Cheryl Pitman's family with the vague feeling that something was wrong with the explanation Richard had given for bringing that woman to their house.

"I'd like to talk to Richard," Kim told Peg, after several sips of the unwanted coffee. She had had two beers with Katherine Senski at Berghof's and felt fairly awash.

"He's sleeping." Peg repeated it as if not sure she had already told Kim.

"I know."

"Kim, he's dead tired. He hasn't been in bed two hours. I couldn't wake him up." She paused. "Is it terribly important?"

Was it important enough to waken an exhausted man to discover whether or not he had been less than candid with her last night? She should be able to live with the thought that Richard had deceived her for a few hours. What difference it made to anything other than her ego it would have been difficult to say. If pride appears, can fall be far behind? But Kim found the thought of returning to Walton Street without having settled her doubts impossible. Sister Mary Teresa was hard enough to live with, but if she were an accomplice with Richard against her, in effect, well . . . Kim told Peg that it was, indeed, important.

Billy had two pie tins he was bringing together with all the fervor of a mad cymbalist, and it seemed to Kim that that alone, forget about the roar of the TV, the throb of the washer, and the constant racket of jets settling down toward O'Hare, should have wakened Richard, even if he had had a long and sleepless night.

"Let me finish my coffee."

Poor Peg. Having that cup of instant coffee with Kim must represent a major respite from her constant chores. Kim told her to take her time. She even accepted the offer of another cup for herself. As she fetched it, Peg took one pie tin away from Billy. He looked up at her, considered the matter, then began to beat on the floor with the remaining weapon. If this bothered Peg, she showed no sign of it.

"I'm surprised Richard didn't sleep right through the shooting last night," Kim said.

"What exactly happened?"

"Didn't Richard tell you?"

"You know Richard, Kim."

Kim knew Richard and how perfunctory an account he would give Peg. So she told her. It was odd how swiftly so hair-raising an event becomes domesticated in the telling. Listening to herself, Kim could almost wonder why she had been scared half out of her wits last night. Perhaps a dozen bullets had come through a bedroom window, continued through the closed door of the room, and ended up in the wall of the hallway outside the bedroom. Ho hum. No one had been struck. The noise had been that of shattering glass and splintering wood.

"So they used silencers," Peg said.

"I suppose they did," Kim replied, deferring to a detective's wife's knowledge of such things.

"And no one was hit?"

"It looks as if it was done just to frighten us. Or rather to scare Cheryl Pitman." Kim found she did not want to repeat the explanation Richard had given her. If that was not the truth or the whole story, she did not want to compound her sense of foolishness by repeating it once again.

"What time was the shooting?"

"Three o'clock."

"Then that wasn't it. It was the busy signal."

"I don't understand."

Peg leaned toward Kim. "I telephoned there last night. At two o'clock. Edward woke up with some sort of a bad dream and after I'd settled him down I lay awake feeling sorry for myself and I thought of Richard over there on Walton Street baby-sitting for this spoiled, rich woman, and I just picked up the phone and dialed. I got a busy signal."

"A busy signal."

"Well, if it had been after three, all that shooting might have knocked your phone out of order. But this was before."

"But who on earth . . ."

"What's the matter?"

Kim had stood up. She didn't want to say. "Let's wake up Richard."

Kim started through the house to the staircase, and Peg came along with her. She was obviously puzzled by the determination with which Kim moved, but Kim wanted Richard to hear about that telephone call and the busy signal and let him have whatever thoughts it prompted him to have.

"Maybe Richard was trying to call me."

Her remark slowed Kim down and she realized that she did not want to admit the possibility that it had been Richard on the phone when Peg tried to call. It had not been Sister Mary Teresa, it had not been Joyce, and it had not been Kim. Now they had to waken Richard in order to exclude him as well. Kim had excluded him without really thinking when Peg's mention of her phone call turned a light on inside her skull that seemed to be the reason for the doubts she had been having.

Richard looked like the wrath of God when Peg got him awake. He stared at her and then at Kim, his eyes unfocused, his hair tousled, his face pale with exhausted sleep.

"Richard," Kim said, "Peg called the house last night. She got a busy signal."

"What are you talking about?"

"The house on Walton Street. Peg telephoned there at two o'clock."

"Eddie had a bad dream and I got up to soothe him," Peg said.

Richard stared at her and then at Kim as if they were both insane.

"The phone was *busy*, Richard. At two o'clock. The phone at Walton Street was busy. Were you using it?"

"At two o'clock in the morning?"

"Then you weren't?"

"No." He dropped back on his pillow and his eyes closed.

"Don't let him fall asleep, Peg. Richard, someone was

using our phone this morning at two o'clock. It wasn't you, it wasn't me. It wasn't Joyce and it wasn't Emtee Dempsey. Who does that leave?"

He rolled his head back and forth on the pillow, his eyes closed. "What the hell difference does it make, Kim?"

"Think about it, for heaven's sake. Sister Mary Teresa said she put on a big performance in order to lead anyone who had our house under surveillance to think Cheryl Pitman was in the guest room. She switched her into her own room. That's where the upstairs phone is!"

Richard opened one eye and looked at Kim.

"So what?"

"That's how they knew which room to shoot at."

Peg was staring too. Kim's expression must have appealed to them to make the connection, but they were unable or unwilling to.

"She told them, Richard. She called them up and told them."

"She directed the fire? Come on."

"You say you know gunmen were involved. What you want to learn is who hired them. She did, Richard."

He said nothing, but he threw back the covers and sat up on the edge of the bed. Peg stood and Kim backed toward the door. That was all she wanted, to lodge the thought in his head. He didn't have to express a reaction, he was going to look into it, she was sure of that. It made sense, but of course it made no sense. If Richard knew more than he had told Kim last night, it obviously did not render ridiculous the thought that had been sparked by Peg's mention of her attempted telephone call to Walton Street at two o'clock last night.

"Aren't you going to wait for Richard to come down?" Peg asked.

"Sister Mary Teresa is waiting for me," Kim said carefully.

Peg made a face. "You're nothing but a babysitter to her."

Kim pointed at the kids. "You should talk."

"That's different."

She was right. It was different. Emtee Dempsey liked to quote Doctor Johnson's remark to the effect that marriage has its pains, but celibacy has no pleasures. Of course, she cited it only to refute it. God knows Peg's life looked a lot more hectic than her own. Besides, Kim was mimicking Sister Mary Teresa rather than jumping up to look after her. *She might be waiting for me, but I do not intend to go straight home.* Ah, the flexibility of the truth. But she felt guilty going out to the car. What difference would it have made if she told Peg she wasn't going back to Walton Street, at least not right away?

Four

Kim took the skyway and then continued on Interstate 90 into Indiana. From a phone booth beyond the toll plaza of the skyway she called Walton Street to explain that she would not be coming directly home.

.   "So who's expecting you?" Joyce asked.

"Hasn't she asked for me?"

"Why so enigmatic? Do you want me to put her on?"

"No! Just tell her I called and I'll be back as soon as I can."

"That's real newsy. She'll like that."

As Joyce spoke, Kim heard another receiver lift, doubtless the one in the study. She hung up as silently and quickly as she could. Not only did she not want to give Sister Mary Teresa an opportunity to send her on another errand, she did not want to tell her of the little epiphany she had had as a result of hearing of Peg's attempt to telephone Walton Street last night. Yet she knew that if she spoke with Sister Mary Teresa she would blurt it out, and what would Emtee Dempsey have to say? Kim supposed she feared the old nun would find some flaw in her inference, or see something she had not yet seen. Kim did not want any obstacle to prevent her going immediately to confront Cheryl Pitman.

If what Kim suspected was true, Cheryl Pitman had jeopardized Sister Mary Teresa and Joyce and herself and had been making fools of Richard and a lot of other policemen.

It was just the sort of self-indulgent capriciousness to be expected of her, Kim decided. Life was a game, she made up the rules, everyone else was manipulable, a possible instrument of her whims. As she drove, Kim's anger mounted. The memory of little Miriam, abandoned in that school on the opposite side of Chicago, seemed to add to the indictment.

Whiting, East Chicago, Gary—there is a string of towns along the lake that seem to have been built according to specifications out of Dante. Great smokestacks send rusty and yellowish clouds of lethal fumes into the air, flames leap in the distance day and night, refineries, steel mills, all of it the stuff of industrial might. But what goes up must come down, and the gunk-filled air spread a gritty film of desolate dust on everything. Nothing sparkled, nothing looked clean. Water, stagnant and viscous, looked like the spillover from caldrons boiling in a madman's massive laboratory. Yet people lived here. On the other side of the highway, rows of houses, identical as sausages, lay under the double burden of the freighted atmosphere and the grime that was the final coat, turning paint into shades of gray. When Kim meditated on purgatory, she thought of that stretch along Lake Michigan. Oh, she was sure that many people lived full and happy lives in those cities which are other than Chicago by little more than a distinction of reason, just as the boundary between Illinois and Indiana is no more significant than a seam in the highway. Kim could imagine the citizens of this area driving through Chicago proper shaking their heads in wonder that human beings should live in such awful conditions, but in Chicago the lake was a great cleanser whose winds freshened the city and whose rains washed it clean. Here the lake seemed only one more source of the general pollution. The area has been dubbed by Chamber of Commerce types with a tin ear Illiana. That neologism was perhaps no sillier than the originals from which it was formed, but it struck Kim as insipid. So too the sign indicating the state line on which the governor welcomed her to Indiana suddenly displeased her and she gave a disapproving frown as she tooled by in the Bug.

The route she went along was one that conjured up memories of vacations and weekend outings both before and after she had entered the convent. Her family had often rented along this shore of Lake Michigan in long-ago summers. A-frames, cottages, places of varying attractiveness, but of course the dwelling did not matter; it was proximity to the water they wanted. They spent all day on the beach, they cooked out, they sat around the picnic table until dark fell and went inside only to drop into bed and oblivion. Kim remembered summers spent in cottages built on a bluff high above the beach, so that they had to go down hundreds of steps to get to sand and water and were correspondingly reluctant to make the climb unnecessarily. They brought a picnic lunch down with them in the morning and stayed on the beach all day.

Now, in spring, as she passed through the short stretch of Indiana and entered Michigan—three states in a matter of minutes—the surroundings did and did not look like the familiar setting of all those happy summer days. Since she had entered religion, she had come along this route to the summer house of the Order of Martha and Mary, another gift from another benefactor, a lovely lake place to which they repaired for at least a month each summer. Sister Mary Teresa grumbled, but came along anyway. Transporting her meant transposing her place of work from Walton Street to the large house just west of Benton

Harbor. No sooner were they settled in than the old nun resumed her work. It was difficult to know what the point was, in her case, of altering the setting in which she simply carried on as before. Would it really matter if they listened to her pleas and left her at her desk in the house on Walton Street? But of course she could not be left alone, which meant that Joyce or Kim or both would have to forego a month at the lake in order to look after her. Kim assured herself that even though the old nun remained housebound she benefited from the healthy air—the lake freshened and the air became invigorating long before the road reached Benton Harbor—but it was difficult to know in what way the air was preferable to that they enjoyed on Walton Street.

Union Pier, Michigan, is named, needless to say, after the pier that juts out into Lake Michigan, and there is a town of sorts that centers around the intersection of the highway and a road that runs roughly westward to the lake and pier and more or less eastward into fruit farms and summer places it would be exaggerated to call estates. This shore has long functioned as one of the places to which wealthy Chicago withdraws from the heat of summer.

A semaphore swung over the intersection like a pendant and perversely remained green when Kim would have welcomed a mandatory stop. Now that she was almost at the house, she was beginning to doubt the theory that had brought her here pell-mell. She slid through the intersection and pulled into an unpaved expanse that served as a parking lot for a low cinderblock building that housed a tavern. In a small window a brand of beer was spelled in glowing neon. What exactly did she plan to do or say when she confronted Cheryl Pitman? Suddenly the two-in-the-morning phone call seemed something that could be explained in a dozen innocuous ways. Besides, once she began to speculate that she was being told less than the truth, she could reasonably doubt that Cheryl had been brought here to their place on Lake Michigan. Of course they had told her that, but wasn't that what made it dubious—if she was going to give free rein to her suspicions? Maybe she should pop into Thatcher's Tavern and ask the boys at the bar if they had noticed a platoon of Chicago police escorting a woman through Union Pier?

For a mad moment she thought of calling Walton Street and talking things over with Sister Mary Teresa. But that would be something she could never live down. If she had acted on a bad hunch, she would be wiser to keep quiet about it. But first she had to see if the hunch was bad. And that meant going the remaining mile to their house.

When she reached the house, traffic in the opposite lane prevented her from making the turn into the driveway immediately. Kim could see the green tile roof of the house clearly though the bare arms of the trees. In summer the presence of the house had to be taken on faith. But, if semi-visible now, the house looked deserted. Finally she was able to make the turn, cross the westbound lane, and, having gone between the stone pillars that supported a wrought-iron crosspiece in which LAKEHAVEN was written, drop down the steep driveway where, within a minute, it might have been a million miles from the busy highway she had just left.

The drive led past the house and on to the great four-stall garage beyond. There was no evidence the house was occupied; there was no sign of another vehicle. But as soon as Kim came to a stop and turned off the motor, her car was surrounded.

The reception committee came from the garage, the house, and the grounds. Kim put up her hands in mock surrender as the men with their grim expressions and the women with their sensible hair-dos and shoes converged on the car. Failing to amuse her encirclers, she rolled down the window.

"Hi! I guess I'm lost." She searched the faces for a familiar one, one she had seen at Walton Street.

"Could I see your driver's license, ma'am?" The man who spoke had come to the side of the car to study her with an expressionless face, but his eyes seemed alert for trouble.

"What's the charge, speeding?"

"Trespassing. Your driver's license, please."

There might have been some amusement to be found in being accused of trespassing on one's own property, but Kim was not tempted by it.

"Let me see *your* identification," she said.

He obliged. He was a policeman, a Chicago policeman named Hanson.

"That's funny. I thought I was in Michigan."

"Would you please get out of the car?"

His polite tone did not deceive her. A hand lifted, palm upward, and his fingers folded into it like a Japanese fan, the gesture bringing a female cohort. There seemed nothing to be gained from delay, so Kim got out of the car. She was replaced behind the wheel immediately and as they started off toward the house, her interlocutor and the summoned female, she heard her car start up again. She turned to see it continue down to the garage and inside.

"Do I get a claim ticket?" she asked her male companion. When he ignored her, she turned to the lady whose pageboy hairdo had an artful streak of gray in it. "What are the parking rates here?" No answer from her either. "Well, it's certainly convenient, I'll say that. Close to all the best stores."

They entered by the kitchen door, continued through the dining room to the parlor, where Cheryl Pitman sat alone on the couch, the low table before her covered with edibles and potables. She sat at one end, her legs drawn up on the couch, and she had been watching the kind of TV program Joyce adored.

"For heaven's sake," she cried, recognizing Kim. "What are you doing here?"

"You look comfy."

Cheryl made a face. "Would you look at that." She pointed with disgust at the TV screen where the picture was doing a slow and vertiginous flip-flop. "The reception here is awful!"

"Oh, I don't know. I had quite a welcoming committee."

Hanson, who seemed to be in charge, asked Cheryl Pitman if she knew Kim, and if so, who she was.

"This is Sister Kimberly."

"Sister Kimberly."

"She's a nun! Aren't you? Tell them."

Her tone was the delighted one of the hostess who has produced not a celebrity, but a curiosity. Kim's escorts seemed to have forgotten how to keep their faces immobile.

One of the more exacting demands of the ecumenical age is that those who find the concept of the religious life as dead as the Dark Ages must behave as if they spend a good part of their day chatting with nuns and monks and find the whole thing as natural as Chaucer. But the male cop looked at Kim with a Protestant wariness he could not suppress, while the female, fleetingly imagining herself in Kim's shoes, actually took a step backward. Did they think Kim would now whip out a vial of holy water and let them have a salvific sprinkle?

"Sister Kimberly Moriarity," she said. "Our house is on Walton Street in Chicago. This is our house too."

Hanson received this news unblinkingly. It was difficult to tell whether he was remembering accusing her of trespassing.

"Her brother is one of you," Cheryl Pitman cried, her bag of goodies not yet empty.

"Eugene?"

"Richard." Chicago is full of Moriaritys. Kim's mother's name was Burke and there are many of those too. That the city was "too Burkeular" was a much-used item in her father's small arsenal of jokes.

"He took care of me last night," Cheryl Pitman said.

It was one remark too many. These public servants clearly were not enjoying playing nursemaid to the Gold Coast heiress who lounged upon the couch, whiling away the day before the TV while they remained anxiously on the alert.

"I'd like to talk to Mrs. Pitman," Kim said.

They could not have cared less. Having established that she was innocuous, known to the object of their concern and, though a nun, not visibly different from anyone else, they withdrew.

Cheryl turned her head a degree or two so her look was slightly askance. "What on earth brings you here, Kim?"

Of all the things she might have said, Kim said the simplest.

"I saw Miriam this morning."

There was a split second during which Cheryl did not seem to know who Miriam might be. In fairness, there was no reason why she would expect Kim to refer to her daughter: for all she knew Kim did not even know she had a child. Nonetheless, that moment during which she appeared oblivious of the wide-eyed child in Birnam School seemed to sum up much of the sadness that can attend the lives even of the very wealthy.

"You *saw* her?" She became alarmed. "But she's supposed to be in school . . . "

"I saw her in school. I drove out there this morning."

"Why?" She had taken her legs off the couch and now rummaged on the coffee table for a pack of cigarettes. She shook one free and put it in her mouth, where it dangled while she searched for a match. Kim had the impression she was waiting for someone to light her cigarette for her. Since Kim was the only one in the room with her now, she would wait a long time indeed. She picked up a lighter, pressed it, did not bring the flame to her cigarette. "Is she all right?"

Again the delay before the reaction that should have been instinctive. In her *Counsels* addressed to the fledgling Order of Martha and Mary, Blessed Abigail Keineswegs, their saintly founder, cautions her daughters in Christ always to show the greatest charity toward the worldling lest they be, however unwittingly, an occasion for the rejection of religion, as are words without corresponding actions. It was part of Kim's religious duty as an M. & M. to read the *Counsels* through carefully once a year. When they read Blessed Abigail in the novitiate they were required to keep a notebook open on the desk before them in which to jot down thoughts on the personal applicability of the *Counsels* to their lives. It was a wise book and one that bore up well under such constant scrutiny. The maxim just cited is wise, it is right, it is Christian through and through. But so is the exhortation to turn the other cheek. The pagan that still lurks in the depths of us all emerged from the dark side of Kim's soul, she resisted the lure of her training and convictions and overt beliefs, and would very much have liked to say something particularly cutting and hurtful, even to slap Cheryl, so that physical pain would force her out of the crustacean shell of egoism she seemed to inhabit.

"She asked about you." It emerged as a simple statement of fact and did not, at least to her own ear, betray her feelings of animosity. Blessed Abigail would be, if not proud of her, at least forgiving.

"For me, it's one of the hardest things not being able to get out there more frequently."

"You do visit her?"

She looked sharply at Kim. "What kind of a question is that?"

Kim imagined Blessed Abigail dropping her veil over her face and withdrawing from the room. Her excuse was that straight talk would be good for Cheryl Pitman's soul. It certainly helped her own.

"Miriam said she seldom sees you."

A martyr's smile. "Children."

"Miriam is your only child, isn't she?"

"Yes." Her answer suggested Kim might have been an investigator from Planned Parenthood.

"It seems a shame for her to be in boarding school."

"On the contrary. It has done her a world of good. Birnam School is an excellent place and Jane Corydon a remarkable woman. Amos discovered the school but the decision to put

Miriam there was mine. Miriam's and mine. Let me tell you something about Jane Corydon. She is an alcoholic."

Kim must have looked surprised. Cheryl Pitman smiled as if she had scored a point.

"I mean, of course, a reformed alcoholic. She is a brilliant woman who very nearly ruined her life but is now on an upward track. She is ambitious, and that is something I understand. She wants money, and I wish her all the luck in the world. She is a perfect role model for Miriam. I want her to look up to a woman with fortitude and drive and a healthy respect for money honorably earned."

"What prevents you from visiting Miriam?"

She attempted a sad smile. "You cannot have, in the seclusion of your convent, a very accurate idea of what life in the real world is like. A person in my position has many demands on her time. My life is not something over which I have absolute control. The comparison I have often used, and I do not mean to be presumptuous, is the English royal house. You know the schedule of the queen, the prince consort, their children, cousins, aunts and uncles—the whole lot of them are in constant movement, opening exhibitions, christening ships, viewing parades, presiding, judging, simply appearing and lending their name. It is much the same with me. I don't know what you know of my family."

"Quite a lot."

"Oh?"

"I had lunch with a newspaperwoman on the *Trib*, Katherine Senski. She gave me an envelope filled with clippings, but, more valuable, an oral account of your great-grandfather and the rest of the family."

Cheryl was flattered, quite obviously, but she was surprised as well. Something of Miriam's watchful look came over her mother's face.

"Why did the subject arise?"

"Because of last night."

"I see. Isn't it rather late to be checking the pedigree of your overnight guest?"

"Sister Mary Teresa asked me to do it."

"What a remarkable woman she is."

"She also sent me to speak to Miriam."

"Do you know I just babbled with that woman? Don't take offense when I say that nuns have never been my favorite people. Your whole way of life strikes me as, well, let's just say I could not live that way. But with her, Sister Mary Teresa, none of that seemed to matter. At the time I think I felt that she was doing all the talking, but afterward I realized it was I who dominated the conversation. Drink will sometimes make me talkative, but I had only a few weak . . . " She let her voice drift away. Her eyes left Kim's, turned to the TV, and kept going to the window. "I would like to talk to her again someday." She turned back to Kim. "She asked you to go see Miriam?"

"Yes."

"I wonder why."

"Perhaps it was something you said to her."

"Perhaps. We talked about everything—my family, my father. Is Chicago your native city?"

"Yes."

"Then you must have heard of my father."

Kim supposed she had. Certainly while she listened to Katherine Senski she had the feeling Katherine was filling in a vague outline rather than starting with a completely blank slate. Like Wrigleys and Fields and so many other Chicago families, she knew Cheryl Pitman's without really knowing it. She could scarcely deny having heard of her father.

"I must have."

"He was a wonderful man." Her eyes locked with Kim's as if this was the first important thing she had ever said to her and she must understand it and see it as Cheryl did. "When I was a girl, he was my idol. He remained my idol until he died. He was good and generous and he took very seriously that view of the family I've mentioned. *Noblesse oblige.* Chicago had been good to us, we must be good in return. That meant never refusing, if it was at all possible to accept them, requests for service, for money, for appearances, anything. And people loved him. Those clippings you got, have you looked at them?"

"Not yet."

"When you do, take special notice of the way the newspapers wrote of him. Adulatory, it's the only word. He was a prince and they saw it and wrote of him accordingly." She was fervent. Clearly she meant every word she was saying, and they simply burst from her. Listening, Kim felt her attitude altering. Cheryl seemed a version of Miriam now, though Kim supposed it would be more accurate to put it the other way around, but Cheryl had had one parent at least who paid attention and returned love with love. It was almost a relief to hear Cheryl express her feelings of love for her father. Not a surprising sentiment, of course, but this was a woman who seemed to have to think in order to remember her only child. No, the sentiment was surprising not in its nature, but in its intensity. Cheryl was not simply telling Kim that others had admired and respected and adulated her father. She had too. She still did. Then why did her face suddenly cloud over as she recalled the triumphant scenes of her father's involvement in the public and social life of Chicago?

"I suppose she gave you clippings of the coverage after he died."

"I suppose so. As I said, I haven't had time . . . "

"It was horrible. They turned on him like snarling dogs after he was dead. This wonderful man, this generous and good man, as their own newspapers had recorded—once he was dead they depicted him as a spoiled scion of a house whose money was tainted to begin with. His gifts were bribes, conscience money; his public appearances efforts to achieve respectability despite his private life. Oh yes, they dredged up largely fictional dirt on his personal life." She drew her lower lip between her teeth, and moved her head back and forth, eyes glistening with tears.

Her voice had been more bewildered than bitter, and Kim could not help thinking that, just as her description of her father's activities might very well be taken as an account of her own days, so her shock at the posthumous treatment her father had received in the newspapers was somehow anticipatory, a dread that she, too, no matter the way she was regarded alive, would be dismissed and patronized in death. For the first time Kim noticed the number of newspapers on the coffee table and on the floor around the sofa. Cheryl Pitman was clearly an avid reader of the newspapers she said had pilloried her dead father.

Kim said, "Your brother Herbert seems to be among the critics of your father."

"Herbert!" Cheryl sat up and her eyes sparked with anger. "Herbert is an ass. What do you know about him?"

"Just what I read in the papers." Kim said ingenuously.

"That isn't the half of it. He would like to take every cent the family has ever earned and just throw it away."

"I understand he gave money to people."

"People! And what kind of people? Derelicts, drunks, prostitutes, other cronies of his."

"I heard about the house too."

Cheryl's eyes narrowed and she inhaled, apparently ready to speak to that point too, but then she stopped. She closed her eyes, tilted her chin, and again inhaled. Kim's sympathy for the woman was hard to retain when she recalled why she had driven directly to Union Pier from Richard's house.

"My sister-in-law tried to telephone our house on Walton Street last night."

Cheryl Pitman's eyes opened and she looked at Kim as if she were mad. She waited as if to hear what absurdity she might utter next.

"She was worried about my nephew and wanted to talk to my brother. Richard Moriarity."

"Yes?" She remembered Richard without an effort.

"She called at two o'clock. The line was busy."

Still she seemed to wait for Kim to say something relevant to their conversation or perhaps simply something that made sense in any way whatsoever.

"The line was busy. Someone was on the phone. It wasn't Sister Mary Teresa. It wasn't Sister Joyce. It wasn't me."

"Then it must have been one of the police."

"It was not one of the police."

How quiet it was in the house. How quiet it was there in the country. Cheryl Pitman looked at Kim steadily, her eyes bright, glistening, but not with tears.

"And you think it was me." She smiled indulgently. "I tried unsuccessfully to pay for my accommodations for last night. Are you now asking reimbursement for a phone call?"

"Then you were on the phone?"

"After your brilliant argument, how could I deny it? By elimination, it must be me. What earthly difference does it make?"

When the noise began, the preceding silence seemed to have been merely a prelude for it, as if they had been waiting for the sound of firing, the sound of smashing glass and wood, the shouts and commotion in the yard. Cheryl Pitman leaped from the sofa, but Kim was already on her feet. A figure came streaking into the room heading straight for Cheryl Pitman. With more or less of a tackle she was pushed back onto the couch and the couch was shoved into a corner of the room. Kim stood watching all this open-mouthed, while the sound of firing continued and upstairs there was the sound of metal pinging, glass shattering, things falling and toppling. And then the silence returned, as complete as before.

The policewoman who had pinned Cheryl Pitman to the couch and in the same motion moved the couch to a safer part of the room pushed herself to her feet and looked toward the door. The male cop who had interrogated Kim and then led her inside the house came into the room.

"She's all right?"

"My God," Cheryl Pitman said. "Again."

"All the shots went upstairs," the woman said.

Outside there was much shouting. Motors started and cars roared past the house, heading for the road. Presumably they were in pursuit of the gunmen.

Kim went to the stairs and started up.

"Hold it," the cop shouted.

"It's over," Kim said, continuing up. "I went through this last night too."

He was at her side before she got to the landing, but he did not try to stop her. At the top of the stairs Kim got her bearings and started down the hallway. The bullet-shattered doorway was more than clue enough. They looked into the room from the hallway. There were enough smashed, broken, and punctured things in that room in which to seek significance. Kim started into the room, but with a hand on her arm, the policeman stopped her.

"Better not. There may be spent slugs lying around. For all we know, they're not done yet."

His words impressed himself, certainly. He started swiftly back down the hallway, gripping Kim's arm. Cheryl Pitman sat on the couch, eyes wide, mouth open, the picture of shock.

Hanson went away. Cheryl patted a spot on the couch beside her, but Kim remained standing. It was all she could do not to blurt out a half-hysterical accusation, an indictment, of this pampered wealthy woman.

"I called my husband last night," Cheryl said in a quiet voice. I wanted to tell him what was happening."

"And where you were?"

"Yes." Cheryl smiled slightly. "It seemed safe enough."

"Did you tell him which room as well?"

Cheryl made a face. "I didn't want to turn on the light

when I dialed. So I let up the shade of the room while I did." She shook her head. "And afterward I pulled it down again."

Ye Gods! She might have been signaling.

Hanson was back. He wanted Cheryl out of that room, away from the side of the house from which the bullets had come. Kim thanked God she had not said more than she had to Cheryl. It was bad enough to think such evil of the poor woman, but it would have been unforgivable to accuse her of so dreadful a thing in the presence of others. Cheryl looked back at Kim as Hanson led her from the room.

"I'm sorry," Kim called after her.

But then Cheryl was gone, though her puzzled expression seemed to remain as an afterimage for a moment.

Kim left the house. There were two other cars in the garage beside her own. The lady cop was in one of them, on the radio, her dispassionate voice recounting what had happened, telling who had gone to investigate the apparent source of the fire.

"They were southeast of the house. They aimed at the upper floor." A pause. "Only the upper floor."

"And at only one room on the upper floor," Kim murmured. How different in significance that remark now was than it would have been before the explanation of the phone call from Walton Street.

The cop ignored Kim. That is, she ignored her until Kim got into the Bug and started its motor. The woman was out of the police car and across the garage to Kim's in record time. She reached in, trying to get the keys. Kim slapped her hand, hard.

The woman's face was inches from Kim's and her eyes swarmed with hostile thoughts. Like the others, she had her badge pinned to her lapel—ID picture, badge number, name. Eileen Harrod. She was the New Woman, bursting from confining boundaries, entering professions hitherto closed to women. There was nothing romantic or even attractive about the role of policewoman that afternoon in a garage in Michigan. She was just a woman exasperated with another woman who refused to do what she was told. The surprise of the slap caused her to step back from the car.

That was when Kim stepped on the gas. As she flew up the driveway, she half expected to be shot at. But that was ridiculous. She was a free woman. Nonetheless, her hands gripped the wheel tightly and her knuckles whitened on the dash to the road.

Back on the highway, she pressed the gas pedal to the floor, as if she could drive away from her stupid suspicion of Cheryl Pitman. Whatever had prompted her to think the woman would actually call down a hail of bullets on houses in which she was defenseless against them? Thank God she had not mentioned her theory to Emtee Dempsey. She would never have heard the end of it.

Why had Cheryl phoned her husband last night? She was supposed to be hiding from him as well as her assailants. The gland of suspicion began again to secrete its fluid into her heart, but Kim put a stop to it at once. Let the police solve the mystery. But she meant to speak to Richard about his claim that the police knew or thought they knew the identity of Cheryl's assailants. If they knew, the men should be arrested. It was crazy to let them run around free. They had found the hiding place on Walton last night and they must have followed the escort into Michigan, no matter how elaborate the plans for deceiving any followers had been devised.

Kim was doing over seventy when she heard the siren and looked into the rearview mirror and saw the state patrol car. They were Michigan police and the Indiana border was mere miles ahead of her. If she had really floored it and gotten across the border into Indiana, would they have had to turn back? The idea seemed no more foolish than most of the others she had had that day. Given her luck so far, she decided not to act on it. What would the headline have been? Speeding Sister Slips Pursuing Police. She pulled to the side of the road and watched in the mirror as the patrol car pulled in behind her.

She waited for the trooper to come to her car. And waited. There were two of them, side by side, looking straight ahead. It occurred to Kim that they were waiting for her. She got out of the car and walked back to them. The door of the patrol car opened, a back door, as she approached.

"Better get inside, Miss. Watch the traffic."

A huge truck passed and she felt blown toward the patrol car. She scampered inside and pulled the door shut after her. She opened her purse to get out her driver's license.

To her surprise, the patrol car began to move. The driver pulled onto the highway, turned on the siren, and started toward Chicago at a mounting rate of speed.

"Hey, what's going on!"

Neither head turned. Maybe she really had become invisible.

But in the pit of her stomach fear formed like a closed fist.

Five

The radio crackled with police traffic and it was from it rather than from the two taciturn troopers in the front seat that Kim received an explanation of her arrest. Despite the electronic distortion, she recognized Eileen Harrod's voice. Her description of Kim was, she supposed, accurate. It certainly was not flattering nor, Kim was sure, was it meant to be. Well, that's what she got for slapping a cop.

"Subject medium height, thirtyish, red hair worn short, straight. Kimberly Moriarity. Roman Catholic nun."

The nondriver turned to look at Kim, his mouth slack. His sunglasses hid whatever reaction registered in his eyes. He exchanged a look with the driver, who was also wearing nearly opaque sunglasses.

"That true?" he asked Kim.

"Yes."

But Eileen was far from through. She mentioned Kim's relationship to Richard as well, and Kim detected an appeal to a professionally received opinion that the relatives of a policeman can be a pain in the neck. Eileen Harrod linked the desire to apprehend Kim with the attacks made on Cheryl Pitman, last night in Chicago, minutes ago in Michigan.

"Your brother's a cop?" The trooper in the passenger seat removed his hat and put an elbow over the back of his seat as he turned toward Kim.

Was it his skepticism she addressed? Was it pride in Richard? Or was it the all-too-human desire to show him she knew more than he did? In any case, she babbled.

"I didn't do it," Kim said, in a doomed effort to be funny. "They know who the gunmen are. Richard told me that. They are quite sure who is doing the shooting and they are trying to find out who is paying them to do it."

"Your brother the cop told you that?"

"That's right."

"Did he tell you their names?"

The sign announcing they were entering Indiana loomed and they sped past. That seemed odd. For that matter, the questions, or the trooper's way of asking them, seemed odd too.

"Where are we going?"

"Not far."

"We're in Indiana now."

The man took his elbow off the back of the seat and turned away. The driver concentrated on his task. Eileen began a repeat of her announcement that a fleeing nun was wanted for questioning, describing Kim's car, giving its tag number. Why had Eileen Harrod let Kim go if she meant to put out a bulletin like that only minutes later? Maybe she had been lambasted by Hanson for letting Kim go. Kim was a witness to what had happened, but then, so were the rest of them. Perhaps it just seemed disorganized to let someone who had been there during the assault drive off as if the party was over and there was no longer any reason to stay.

"They missed again," Kim said, almost sorry to have lost the trooper's attention.

In the rearview mirror, the lenses of the driver's sunglasses seemed fixed on her. But it was the set of his head rather than those uninformative reflecting surfaces that gave Kim the impression she was telling him something he already knew.

Perhaps two miles after they had crossed into Indiana, the patrol car slowed and they pulled off the road, toward the lake, into an area known for its sand dunes. The other car was parked behind a large mound of sand that wore weeds on its brow, a sort of native American motif. Well, after all, this was Indiana. The driver pulled up next to the parked car, which was empty. After he had turned off the motor and got out, he tossed his trooper hat onto the seat before closing the door and opening Kim's. That was when she saw that the hats were all the uniform either of the men had been wearing.

"Let's go."

"No!"

"Please, no violence. You won't be harmed. I may want you to telephone your brother to give him some instructions. If he's cooperative, I'll be too. Come on. Upsy daisy."

Kim had read, and had had read to her, the lives of many saints. In the novitiate they had been read to at the noon meal from a work called the *Martyrology*, which contains accounts of the deaths of those saints whose feast was celebrated that day, saints who had died for their faith. The years of persecution under the emperors provided most of the entries in the work. Kim and the others had learned to go on eating and almost enjoying their food while the more horrendous tortures, prolonged and painful deaths, were being read about in a quavering voice by one of their number. They took turns reading. To stand at the lectern was as unreal as to sit at a table listening, or not listening. One read words, anxious not to make a mistake, scarcely attending to their meaning. Sometimes Kim had asked herself what the point of such reading was, aside from preventing conversation at table. That afternoon on the dunes of Indiana she received what she took to be a partial answer.

She got out of the car and allowed herself to be marched to the other car. The right front door was opened for her and she got in. One of the men got in the back, the other got behind the wheel. Their sunglasses reminded her of a half-forgotten movie featuring Haitian hitmen. She thought of the driver as Nero and the man in the back seat as Diocletian. She opened her hand on her lap and was sure she was going to receive the palm of martyrdom. (It was always called that, the palm of martyrdom. "You've got to hand it to them," was Joyce's explanation. How melancholy humor seems *sub specie aeternitatis*.) Kim just sat there. Docile. Resigned. A young maiden of Rome at the mercy of the emperor's henchmen, on the way to the Coliseum and certain death. Her thoughts sailed on, beyond the arena and the bloodthirsty shouts of the crowd, to the heavenly crown promised those who lay down their lives in witness of their faith. That is what had attracted her during those readings. At least it had attracted her in the novitiate when she was young.

Now, as the car pulled away from the abandoned Michigan State Patrol car and went out to the highway and headed toward Chicago, Kim remembered her youthful thoughts, adding to them the more mature one that it would be futile for her to struggle and protest. She must stay alert and seek her chance. Besides, she was almost curious as to where she was being taken. The mention of a call to Richard seemed a sort of promise that, in the end, all would be well.

"You're not policemen," she said.

There was a snort from the back seat from Diocletian, but Nero stared impassively ahead.

"So you stole that police car."

No answer. She had not expected one. Why had these men stolen a patrol car? Why had they hidden a car there among the dunes? And why on earth had they taken her prisoner?

"How long have you known Mrs. Pitman?" Kim surprised herself with the matter-of-fact tone of her voice.

The driver ran his tongue around inside his mouth for a moment, then said, "Who's Mrs. Pitman?"

"The woman they were talking about on the police radio."

"That's you."

"The other one. The one who was shot at. Twice."

"We don't know anything about it," said Diocletian from the back seat.

"Shut up," Nero advised him.

"Last night she was shot at while staying with us on Walton Street. In Chicago. Today she was shot at in a home we own on Lake Michigan. There are Illinois plates on this car."

"That's where we stole it." Diocletian chuckled as he said this, but Nero frowned.

"I said shut up."

As if the command had been addressed to her, Kim closed her mouth and looked out her window. They were passing through purgatory again. Was her life in danger? It was difficult to think so even in the menacing company of Diocletian and Nero. If they were from Chicago, Richard could very well know who they are, but what comfort was there in that? He said the police had a good idea who had been hired to shoot at Cheryl Pitman and that had not stopped them from firing at her twice. No, not at her. They had a way of missing. Nero and Diocletian looked as if they would have difficulty hitting a target too.

And suddenly the thought was in her mind. Nero and Diocletian were the gunmen! Last night they had fired on the house on Walton Street, they were just returning from their assault on the M. & M.s' lake home in Michigan. Kim no longer felt unmenaced. These men would have picked up Eileen Harrod's description and decided to act on it like good cops. Why?

Kim began to develop a feigned interest in the traffic going in the opposite direction, her eye following a car or truck until it got even with the hood of the car she was in, then turning her head forward again. She continued to increase the angle to which she turned her head until it seemed natural to turn completely and look at the man in the back seat. He had turned too, apparently watching the vehicle of her choice out of sight.

"Turn around," the driver said.

"Would one of you at least say something? Threaten me. Tell me where we're going. Tell me who you are. Something! I hate this silence."

For answer, the driver snapped on the radio. WBBM. Constant news and chatter. Thank God it was past the time of day when Bob and Betty were on. Two males were reading news items, taking turns with each other and with commercial breaks. Soon there would be traffic reports from an observer high in Sears Tower. Chicago radio stations vied with one another to give commuters bird's-eye views of the toll roads and freeways. Most of them relied on helicopters and one could imagine dozens of competing choppers hovering over expressways and interchanges, engaged in dogfights as they sought to be first to report delays, accidents, bottlenecks, road repairs, and all the various impediments that can add a minute or two to one's passage into or out of the city.

The two announcers were philosophizing in an ad-lib way and it was a moment before Kim began to pay attention. They were discussing a report that had just come in from one of the station's reporters. The driver slowed the car and turned up the volume. With the cheery anonymous inflections that go as well with reports of disasters and earthquakes as with pleasant items, the two men were discussing the statistical improbability of two events occurring at the same time.

"The mother was being kept in a lake house in Michigan in protective custody. The daughter is a student at a school west of Glen Ellyn. The daughter is doing as well as can be expected, according to a spokesman at the Loyola University Medical School."

Antiphonically, his partner chimed in. "The attack on Mrs. Pitman last night took place right here in Chicago. Police will not confirm that was the reason for moving Mrs. Pitman to the house in Michigan. Our correspondent Leon Howard is on the line now with the headmistress of the daughter's school. Go ahead, Leon."

And then, incredibly, the voice of Jane Corydon and that of her excited interviewer filled the car. Miriam had been injured.

"Was it gunshot, ma'am?"

"Good heavens, I never thought of that."

"What exactly happened?"

"She was riding. A horse. It panicked and ran. The child was thrown. Why did you mention gunshot?"

"Because of the mother. You've heard of the two attacks on her?"

Jane Corydon gained control of her own excitement and of the conversation. She would not, she said frostily, speculate about such matters. Her pupils and their parents had a right to her discretion and confidence and she did not propose to abuse them.

The program returned to the studio, and the driver turned up the volume louder still.

Kim said, "Your partners weren't as careful as you, were they? Would you have shot at a child?"

"Shut up."

"Don't speak to me like that! It is bad enough shooting up two of our houses without . . ."

He hit her. The driver. His hand whipped out from the wheel and made a great arching movement in a blur and struck her face with an audible sound, but it was the pain and burst of color she noticed. Her head snapped back and bounced off the headrest. The driver's hand remained at the point where it had contacted her face and Kim got a second slighter slap when she bounced forward. Outraged, she pushed the hand away and turned in her seat to face the monster. He kept his arm up between them, his attention on the radio. Two hands gripped Kim's shoulders from behind and pulled her back against the seat.

"We want to hear the news," Diocletian said calmly, reasonably.

They had already heard what interested them, but the repetition of items consequent upon having two broadcasters competing with each other to be witty or profound meant giving the basic facts again and again. Not only had Mrs. Cheryl Pitman been shot at twice during the past twenty-four hours, her daughter Miriam had been injured in a fall from a runaway horse. That the last had been caused by gunfire was a possibility being actively pursued.

"When did it happen?" Nero demanded with angry intensity. "When was the kid injured?"

"The carefully synchronized attacks took place within ten minutes of each other," the radio said, as if in response to his question.

"Ha."

"You are our witness," the man in the back said.

"To what? Kidnaping? Assault?"

"Did anyone force you into this car?"

"You're kidding. And you struck me."

"Forget that. I'm sorry. You want to get out? I'll let you out right here."

They were on the rising approach to the skyway, not exactly a pedestrian's paradise. Kim realized that she had been thinking of getting out of the car when it stopped at the toll plaza of the skyway. There would be a crowd, there would be guards, there were shelters to which she could scamper in seconds. Semiconsciously she had been planning this heroic escape;

now, consciously, she realized she was slightly disappointed to be told she would be allowed to go free. But only slightly. She did not believe the offer so casually made.

"My car is miles back in Michigan."

"We'll take you to it," the man in back said. He hesitated. "Later. We got to be careful. You appreciate that."

"The point is," the driver explained, "you know we weren't there." He took off his glasses. It seemed to change everything. Kim turned and the man in back took off his sunglasses too. It was like finding herself with two new strangers rather than the familiar ones who had just driven her from Michigan.

"My name is Sister Kimberly. People just call me Kim."

"His name is Orville," the driver said.

"Orville what?"

There was the suggestion of the beginning of a twinkle in his eye. "Kimberly what?"

"You already know. Moriarity."

"Right. Orville Rollins."

"His name is Mike Skinner," Orville said.

Mike said, "I'm sorry I hit you. I wanted to hear that item on the radio. You can understand that. You know we weren't anywhere near that kid when someone took a shot at her."

"What difference does that make?"

"What difference does it make!" They had completed the climb and were approaching the toll plaza. Mike swung to the left and into the parking area near the coffee shop. When he had brought the car to a stop, he turned off the motor.

"Want some coffee, Sister?"

"Sure."

Kim reached for the handle of her door and discovered there wasn't any. Mike saw her surprise. "Just a precaution. Let her out, Orville."

"Right."

Inside, in a booth, over mugs of coffee, they took turns trying to convince her they had had nothing to do with the apparent attempt on the life of Miriam Pitman.

"Look, you've seen our work. Did anyone get hurt? No. Was anyone meant to get hurt? No. We wouldn't have taken the job under those conditions. Right, Orville?"

"You're damned right. Sorry." He pointed at the ceramic disc Kim wore on a thong around her neck. "Is that supposed to tell people you're a nun?"

"I don't have to tell people anything, do I?"

"You know what I mean."

"It's a religious medal." The ceramic circle featured tongues of flame, a symbol of the Holy Spirit. "And I do wear it because I'm a nun."

"You know Saint Casey's?"

"Sure." St. Casimir's was a parish on the near south side.

"I went to school there. I had nuns for teachers." He stopped; he was gong to say more and decided not to. Kim sensed an implicit comparison between herself and the nuns of his youth and guessed she did not come out the winner of that one. The theory behind exchanging the habit for ordinary women's clothes—with which she sometimes wore a veil—was that this would erase a barrier between religious and laity, they would confide in nuns, feel more comfortable with them, perhaps be influenced for the better by freer contact with them. And, of course, nuns were expected to gain as well. The results, as Sister Mary Teresa would insist, had been mixed. Of one thing Kim was certain that April afternoon as the rays of the setting sun illumined the skyline and she sat sipping coffee with two self-confessed gunmen: If she wore the traditional habit, she would not be there. She would not have been slapped, she would not now be nearly fifty miles from her car. What were the gains? A free cup of coffee. And these men did speak freely enough to her, though their eloquence was largely a matter of self-pleading.

"To return to the point of the conversation," Mike said. "We had nothing to do with the attack on the kid."

"Friends of yours?"

"How do you mean?"

"Men hired as you were hired. You *were* hired, weren't you?"

"We don't work for nothing."

"Hired by Mrs. Pitman?"

"Look, the important thing is that we were not hired by anybody to shoot that kid, the one who got hit. We would never do that."

"That's true, Sister, it is."

"Why did Mrs. Pitman want you to shoot at her?"

"You got a good look at us. You know our names. You know you were with us when someone shot at that kid. You are our alibi."

"Do I also know you were hired by Mrs. Cheryl Pitman to fake an attack on her, that you shot up our house on Walton Street and that farmhouse bedroom this afternoon?"

"What do you mean, our house?"

"The house on Walton. I live there."

Orville's pasty face seemed to grow paler. "You mean it's a convent?"

"Well, we live there, three nuns. There's a chapel."

"Oh, my God. That's a sacrilege. She didn't tell us that. Nobody would have known."

"It was wrong whether or not it's a convent."

"Wrong, maybe, but not sacrilege. Why, that's like hitting a priest or . . ." He stopped and pointed a finger at Mike. "You done it twice, buddy. You hit a nun."

Orville seemed to have absorbed all the more superficial aspects of a Catholic education. Such arcane points as the canon law on striking religious was not the moral code he needed to get clear on. Despite Mike's reiterated protest, Kim found it difficult to believe they had never used their skill to hit people. She doubted there would be much of a demand for shooting to miss. Was she having coffee with hired killers? Had she ever doubted it? The repetition she could not ignore was that they had nothing to do with the shooting near Glen Ellyn. Of course, she knew they had not been there physically, but that did not prove that other members of their gang or group, what ever it was, had not carried out that part of the day's assignment. But why would they make such a fuss about their noninvolvement if they had, indeed, been involved? They had all but admitted they had twice taken target practice at buildings that housed Cheryl Pitman and they had not disputed her claim that they had been hired to do this by the supposed target of armed wrath.

"If she hired you, she could have hired others to scare her daughter."

They had nothing to say to that. Was it loyalty to their employer, or merely that they did not see how this possibility affected their own case, particularly since they began with the assumption that they were not involved in the attack on Miriam? Their interest was to exonerate themselves, not to implicate her.

"Listen, go to the police and tell them what you were hired to do and what you were not hired to do."

They both sat back. If they had been on chairs instead of the benches of a booth, they would have pushed away from the table, further to dissociate themselves from the suggestion that they voluntarily drop by a police station.

"If they ask us, we'll talk to them, particularly since you can tell them we had nothing to do with the kid. Maybe they don't need to talk to us."

They stood, together, and Orville took a bundle of bills from his pocket and peeled off the outer one like a grocer making a head of lettuce more presentable and dropped it on the table. It was a fifty-dollar bill. Kim picked it up, curious. She had not seen many fifty-dollar bills. Indeed, that might have been the first one.

"Take a cab," Mike said.

"To your car," Orville added.

"Wait." Kim struggled out of the booth, but the two men moved with alacrity, across the café, out the door, to their car. They were spinning out of the parking lot by the time she got to the door. She felt foolish, and the feeling was not diminished by the realization that half the people in the café had witnessed her running after the two men. It seemed wisest to continue on outside. She went down the arrowhead island that tapered off gradually and pointed to the tollbooth where there was a telephone. She put the fifty-dollar bill in her purse and went to the phone booth.

The time was now after six. As she listened to the phone ringing at Walton Street, she could imagine the scene there, Joyce in the kitchen preparing the evening meal, Sister Mary Teresa in her study, doing a final lick of work before calling it quits for the day. There was a phone in the study as well as in the kitchen, but Joyce was far more likely to answer. The phone rang on and on and neither of them answered. Strange. Kim just let the phone ring and the sound of it seemed angry as it continued, scolding Joyce and Emtee Dempsey for ignoring it. She had started to hang up when the phone was answered. She clamped the receiver back to her ear.

"Hello, hello. This is Kim."

After a pause, the voice of Sister Mary Teresa sounded in pensive tones. "Nooo. I don't think so."

"What's going on? What took you so long to answer?"

"That's right. The Order of Martha and Mary."

Kim frowned at the passing traffic. This was like overhearing a conversation rather than taking part in one.

"Can you hear me?"

"That's true."

"Sister, I am at the toll plaza of the skyway. I'm going to take a cab from here, when I can find one. I'll be late."

"That's fine."

"Sister, can you hear me?"

"Yes, I can."

"Someone's there."

Sister Mary Teresa sighed and Kim felt like a fool. "Yes."

"And I shouldn't come home right now."

There was the sound of another receiver being lifted from its hook. Kim replaced hers and stood for a moment in the phone booth, watching the cars go past endlessly. Where was everybody going? She picked up the phone again and called for a cab.

Six

With apparent corroboration of what she had already told Richard, Kim took a cab to her brother's precinct station in the expectation of being greeted there by squads of relieved policemen. Her reception was not quite that.

First of all, she had to sit for forty-five minutes in the squad room, an unwilling witness to dozens of unsavory little vignettes before she was even certain Richard had been told she was waiting to see him. A little harmless nepotism, that. Why not put the admissions of Orville Rollins and Mike Skinner into Richard's hands? No doubt some benefits would befall the one who solved this prickly case, and quite apart from his being her brother, Richard had been put in charge of it. He had been too sleepy and annoyed when she had stood beside his bed and told him the suspected significance of Peg's getting a busy signal when she tried to call the house on Walton Street the previous night.

When Kim first sat down in the squad room she was

tired but exultant, hugging her big secret to herself, dying to see the expression on Richard's face when she told him what she had learned. But a sense of triumph, no matter what the cause of it, could not survive fifteen minutes in that squad room.

Second, there was Richard's actual reaction, no longer dismissible as due to exhaustion and crankiness.

"They just came right out and told you, huh?" A little smile played at the edges of his mouth and Kim recognized the tone from childhood encounters.

"Don't you believe me?"

"Sure I believe you. Knowing Rollins and Skinner, I could hardly doubt you. If I ever knew two people more bent on making a success of their lives, putting the sad past behind them, and . . . "

"Richard!"

"I imagine they confessed to you in your capacity as a nun. Nuns do hear confessions nowadays, don't they?"

"That isn't funny, Richard. In fact, it borders on the sacrilegious."

"You mean I'm trespassing on your territory?" He leaned toward Kim and his eyes sparked with real anger. "Kim, I don't appreciate your sticking your nose into police business. I don't like the suggestion that while we have been standing here with a finger in our ear, intrepid little you has been running around northern Indiana doing our work for us."

"Now, just a minute." Kim got to her feet and her Irish was up too. "Just a darn minute. You were the one who brought that woman to our house last night. Thanks to you, our upstairs was turned into a shooting gallery. Our house in Michigan was turned into a shooting gallery this afternoon. In both cases Orville and Mike were the ones who did it. They told me so. They did it because Cheryl Pitman asked them to."

He turned away and pulled out a package of cigarettes, but Kim took hold of his arm and turned him back to face her.

"The reason they told me was they wanted me to

vouch for the fact that they could not have been the ones who shot at Miriam Pitman. Now, Richard, listen to me. Those two men may be innocent of the attack on Miriam, but is her mother? That is what you have to find out. That is what is important. It is bad enough that she ordered the shooting up of our houses, endangering lives; it is something . . . "

Kim stopped. She had run out of air. Whenever she got angry and tried to talk, she quickly used up all the air in her lungs and didn't seem to take any in. Sentences had a way of ending on a strangled note. They lost any power their content should give them and only caused alarm. Certainly she had captured the attention of everybody there in the squad room.

Third, was the awful session with the state's attorney.

There really was no point in her numbering these things. They were all important, and she wasn't even getting their chronological order right, let alone their relative significance.

But really, that squad room! When they were instructed on how to meditate back in the novitiate they were asked to conjure up scenes to make vivid the point of the spiritual life they meant to ponder. That is how Gary and that stretch of Indiana came to provide Kim with an image of purgatory, but it was a place devoid of people, a setting. Any casting of people for that scene would have to take into account the squad room of a police precinct station.

Kim had been told to sit in a chair beside a desk; it was a hard chair and the desk looked as if lumberjacks had been stomping about on it, but there were four other such desks there in the room, two of them occupied when she sat down. In one chair matching hers was a black woman with what would once have been called a brazen air, but it was her vocabulary that nearly lifted Kim to her feet again before she had settled into her chair. It appeared that she was accused of having stolen the wallet of a man while presumably performing some sexual service for him. The circumstances were gone into in detail, at the top of her voice, and Kim felt the blood rise in her cheeks.

In another chair, a young man sat crouched forward, a long greasy pony tail hanging down the back of his T-shirt. The cop who was interviewing him wore a look of perpetual disgust.

"You haven't begun to feel it, Willie," he promised. "You know how bad it's going to get? So why don't you tell me where you sold it, okay?"

Willie moaned in reply and seemed to fold up further into himself. His interlocutor shook his head in disgust. Patches of perspiration were visible on Willie's T-shirt. Kim no longer worried about the black woman's plight embarrassing Willie. Embarrassment, surprise, even curiosity about the dozen minor tragedies that subsequently unfolded there in the squad room seemed, in such a setting, completely out of place. It might have been a corner of hell if one could have seen these people as without a hope of redemption.

This is the real world, Kim told herself, but immediately she pushed the thought away. She could not bring herself to believe these moral casualties were at all typical of the race. Surely they were the exceptions. But she remembered talks with Richard in which he had suggested that a cop's view of his neighborhood and city is the accurate one and it is not a pretty picture that he sees. And, of course, that had to be true. Who of us does not successfully conceal from others the worse side of herself? So Kim let the thought come back. The squad room was a fair sample of the real world. These broken people were not strangers, alien to herself. They were brothers and sisters, the only difference being that their weakness and sin had become public. And this was the world the Order of Martha and Mary professed itself eager to live in.

Kim welcomed the distraction of wondering what on earth had been going on at Walton Street when she had called there from the toll plaza. It did not seem a weakness to want to telephone again, tell them where she was, ask how they were. Of course, what she wanted, and what she needed, was the reassurance that the sane schedule of the house continued, that the real world also contained people like Joyce and Sister Mary Teresa.

"Dial 9," Willie's tormentor shouted after Kim had tried unsuccessfully to reach the house on Walton. "Dial 9 for an outside line."

Kim hated to be indebted to him even for that. He spoke now to the accompaniment of Willie's moaning protests, the results she learned later of withdrawal from the many drugs to which the boy was addicted. The sound of Joyce speaking in her ear seemed to put her into contact with a lost sanity.

"Where are you?" Joyce demanded.

"At the police station."

"Too bad. So they finally nailed you. Don't worry, we'll hire a good mouthpiece."

"Joyce! Stop it. It isn't funny."

"Are you in trouble?"

"No." She let the monosyllable follow its own echo into silence.

In the squad room a claim not to be in trouble seemed like an impossible luxury. "Why was Emtee Dempsey so mysterious when I called earlier?"

"Because," interrupted the voice of Sister Mary Teresa, "we had guests in the house. Are you serious that you are now at the police station?"

In other circumstance, Kim might have been shaken to realize (a) that she had referred to Sister Mary Teresa by her nickname in her hearing and (b) that the old nun recognized it. But these sank to a satisfying level of triviality at the moment. The reason Sister Mary Teresa, and Joyce too, had reacted as they had to her saying where she was phoning from was that the police had come to Walton Street to question her about the injury to Miriam Pitman.

"Because I visited her at school. Of course." Mysterious caller at Birnam School, self-described author who is actually a nun. "It was your idea, my being Miss Moriarity."

"Was it? I am trying to recall when I last heard you refer to yourself as Sister Kimberly Moriarity."

"Or to you as Dr. Dempsey?"

"How did they find you?"

So Kim told her what had really brought her to the police, at least she gave a version of her reasons. She told her of Orville and Mike, but left out their telling her they had been hired by Cheryl Pitman. Sister Mary Teresa wanted to know if the gunmen had turned themselves in. Kim explained that their main concern was not to be accused of the attack on Miriam.

"How is she, by the way?" Kim asked.

"In the hospital. You must go see her."

"Yes."

How infinitely preferable that seemed to remaining there in the squad room waiting for Richard. After she had promised to return to Walton Street as quickly as she could, and to telephone in an hour in any case, Kim interrupted the cop who was trading obscenities with the prostitute and asked if Richard Moriarity knew she was here waiting for him.

"Sure, sure. He's on his way." His eyes shifted as he lied. Had he picked up the traits of the people with whom he must deal or was his dishonesty something he had brought to his job?

Kim made another phone call. To Peg. Richard was not home. Peg thought she was demented to ask. He had been home all afternoon, as Kim very well knew.

"Did he say anything about why we woke him up?"

"We? I wanted to let him sleep. We should have."

"Then he didn't say anything about your telephone call to Walton Street last night?"

Not that Peg remembered. Kim could imagine the hectic exchanges between them, over the babbling of the children. He probably spared Peg talk about his job in much the same way she would spare Richard all the annoying details of her day. Kim felt foolish for bothering her with these questions. After she hung up, she still had fifteen minutes to wait.

Richard's reaction to what she had to tell him did not make the wait worthwhile. After the initial exchange, after the point where Kim ran out of air, Richard took her by the upper arms as she seemed to turn apoplectic.

"Okay, Kim. Okay. I admit it. I brought you into this mess. But why the hell did you have to go to Union Pier? That was dumb. This is a serious business, and when you just drive into an armed camp, well . . . "

"I had to see her."

He shook his head. "Because a phone was busy? Kim . . . "

She closed her eyes and shook her head. He wanted to lecture her on police procedure, routine, the unreliability of intuition. But her wrong guess about the phone call had not falsified the hunch she had had about Cheryl Pitman.

"Can't we talk in another room?"

Richard looked around the squad room and she realized he did not find it odd. Well, surgeons get used to cutting into people and an operating theater would put her into a dead faint. But then Richard seemed to see the room with her eyes.

"They shouldn't have had you wait here," he growled. "This is for suspects."

"I'm one. Police came to Walton Street to question me about what happened to Miriam Pitman."

"The kid? What would you know about her?"

"I went to see her."

Richard stared at her for a moment, then crossed the squad room and whispered to the Grand Inquisitor. When he came back, he pulled out a chair but did not sit down.

"The headmistress mentioned you had been out there. I don't blame her. She was asked if anything unusual had occurred at the school recently. Nothing but a nosy nun quizzing the little girl who was injured later in the day." Richard shook his head.

"Is there somewhere I could get some coffee and maybe something to eat?"

"Haven't you had supper?"

It was after seven, and although Kim had not eaten, she could scarcely think of herself as embarked on a black fast. Nonetheless, she was ravenously hungry and found the greasy hamburgers available a half block away as tasty as anything of Joyce's. It was in the restaurant, over a second cup of coffee, that she first felt Richard took seriously what she was saying about Cheryl Pitman. For a supposedly cynical policeman, he seemed to have a great deal of trouble imagining Cheryl Pitman capable of such a thing. When it occurred to him that, if what Kim suggested was true, Cheryl Pitman had made a fool out of him, he became angry.

"Orville Rollins and Michael Skinner." Richard shook his head.

"I've got to get back to Walton Street."

"Not yet," Richard said. "Come back with me and give all this to a stenographer and we'll put out a bulletin on Rollins and Skinner."

"They had nothing to do with Miriam Pitman."

"If they've been shooting up places, that's charge enough."

"Maybe they know who Cheryl Pitman hired to go to Birnam School."

They were on their way back to the station when Richard stopped on the sidewalk. He worked his tongue around the inside of his mouth for a moment, then squinted at Kim.

"Kim, forget about trying to link Mrs. Pitman to those gunmen."

"Forget it? How can I?" Kim stopped. "Do you know something I don't know?"

"About who hired them? No. But if it was her, I want no part of it. Neither will the state's attorney. Can you imagine trying to prosecute someone for an attempt on her own life via a third party? What the hell is the motivation supposed to be?"

At this point, Kim would have admitted later, she took unfair refuge in feminine subterfuge. She pretended to be speechless with rage and anger that Richard should suggest Cheryl Pitman might go unpunished for having hired people to shoot at her and, no doubt, at her daughter as well. The thought was more than sufficient to produce outrage, but it did not explain her infuriated look at Richard and turning on her heel before they could reenter the precinct station. She was a model of righteous indignation when she stepped into the cab providentially appearing at just that moment. She did not once look back at Richard. And all the way to Walton Street she pondered the question he had put.

What was Cheryl Pitman's motivation for hiring gunmen to shoot at her and at her daughter as well?

Sister Mary Teresa, pouring cocoa, considered the question. "You mean, beyond the enjoyment of the commotion she has created?"

"Surely that can't be the answer."

Sister Mary Teresa made a little face. She might have been reacting to the smell of cigarette smoke that drifted from the kitchen, but it was Kim's inadequate appreciation of the complexities of human weakness that disappointed her.

"If virtue can be its own reward, so, too, can vice," she mused, with a cup of cocoa held beneath her chin. "Why should we think evil is utilitarian? Besides, boredom is a powerful motive and you must have caught some glimpse of how empty a life that woman's is. Imagine, all but ignoring her daughter. That suggests a dissociation from ordinary attachments and bonds."

"Is that what you learned of her during your long talk?"

The old nun sipped her cocoa. Afterward, she dabbed at her lips with a napkin.

"No. That is why I wanted you to speak with the daughter. I gather you did not find the time to go to the hospital."

"No, I didn't." How guilty this admission made her feel.

"In the morning."

Kim stood in the door of the room watching Miriam before she went in. The child lay on her back, covers pulled to her chin, a pale face on a snow-white pillow staring impassively at the wall. After a moment Kim felt guilty watching her like that, but to back away and then return as if she had just arrived would hardly have been an improvement. Besides, it was difficult not to wonder what was going though Miriam's mind as she lay there alone. Surely an injured child had a right to expect she would be surrounded by concerned friends and relatives. The sight of the abandoned little girl was another reason to fume at Cheryl Pitman. Why wasn't she here? And then Kim realized that Miriam had noticed her.

"Come on in," she said.

"Do you remember me?"

Miriam made a face. "Of course."

"I'm so sorry about what happened to you."

"I'll be all right."

"Do you want to talk about it?"

"Sure."

"What exactly did happen?"

"I was thrown, that's all. My ankle twisted in the stirrup and there is a hairline fracture, but it's the scrapes and bruises I'm in here for."

"What frightened the horse?"

Miriam shrugged. "Who knows? It was Flora."

"Flora."

"A mare. Usually she's so tame she's no fun at all. But every once in a while she decides to act up."

"Did you hear a shot?"

Miriam sat forward, as if Kim meant the question to refer to the present.

"I meant when the horse threw you."

"Did somebody shoot at me? The way they did my mother?"

"You tell me. Dr. Corydon . . . " Kim paused, trying to

remember just how that WBBM radio interview had gone. Jane Corydon had not mentioned any shooting, it was the interviewer who had.

"I'll bet that's what it was," Miriam said excitedly. "Why else would Flora act the way she did?"

"But you didn't hear anything?"

Miriam narrowed her eyes as she searched her memory. Seated on the edge of the bed, Kim could not resist taking the child in her arms. She did not want to encourage her to remember something that had not happened. It was the second time her suspicions of Miriam's mother had run into obstacles.

"Has your mother been to see you?"

"Twice. With my father."

"That's wonderful."

But in a dark corner of her heart Kim resented Cheryl Pitman's having had maternal sense enough to come see her wounded daughter. By her father, Miriam would mean Amos Pitman, who was her foster-father, the husband Cheryl was estranged from.

"She cried and said I had brought them together again."

"What did he say?"

"Amos never says much. But he likes me. He doesn't have to talk."

Kim had brought her a magazine and some candy and some of Joyce's homemade cookies. Miriam asked if the food was from the convent and when Kim said yes seemed glad to have it.

"I bought the candy."

"But not the cookies?"

"No. Sister Joyce baked those."

Miriam scooted to a sitting position and looked at Kim, her face animated with curiosity. "How many are you? Tell me about your life."

So she did. As she spoke, Kim seemed to see it from the inside where she was, but at the same time from without, through the eyes of Miriam Pitman. How odd it must sound to her. She remembered the shocked expression on Miriam's mother's face when Richard brought her to the door. Could Kim go back far enough in her own experience to discover a time when she would have found the lives of nuns strange and foreign? And fascinating, too, as Miriam clearly did. Surely she herself had had similar feelings the first time she sat in a classroom presided over by a woman of indeterminate age wearing a strange costume, little more than a sample of her face showing. But no matter how hard Kim tried to depict that legendary nun in unsympathetic terms, she could not rediscover any sense of the strangeness of religious women. They had been part of her life almost since the dawn of consciousness, and she might just as easily try to conjure up a basic wonderment at the human species itself.

"Do we really sound so bizarre?"

"I meant to ask you about that."

"About what?"

"Bizarres. Do nuns wear them?"

Fortunately, she could not keep a straight face as she asked her question. For answer, Kim twisted her nose, an old nun's trick with naughty children. But she was giggling too. Even atrocious puns were welcome from Miriam Pitman as relief from her seemingly constant solemn attitude. She squirmed away from Kim, laughing aloud herself, crying over her shoulder, "Well, do they?"

Kim was saved from answering by the appearance of a somewhat startled nurse. She got to her feet and stepped away from the bed to let the nurse by. The nurse put a thermometer in Miriam's mouth and said, "And how are we today?"

Miriam answered with a murmur, or it could have been a moan. Kim said, if only to save Miriam more inane questioning, "I'm Sister Kimberly."

"I know."

"You know? But how could you ..."

"Your superior called the nurses' station."

"Sister Mary Teresa?"

"She said her name was Joyce. You're to call home."

Kim called Walton Street from a phone in the hospital, curious to ask Joyce when she had been made superior. But Joyce was uncharacteristically serious.

"A man named Drew called, from the state's attorney's office. Something like that. Anyway, it sounded important, he wanted you to get in touch with him right away. About Cheryl Pitman. He left a number."

Kim called the number next and had to wait three minutes before being put though to Mr. Drew. The girl who answered asked if she would hold, and when Kim said she would, her ear was suddenly filled with Muzak. She held the receiver away from her ear, but close enough to hear when the music stopped and the *vox humana* began. There was no way to avoid the awful music.

"Drew speaking."

"Did you know that people who call you have to listen to music while they wait for you to come to the phone?"

"Who is this?"

"Kim Moriarity. Sister Kimberly Moriarity."

"Oh, yes, yes. You don't like our music?" A subdued chuckle got into his tone.

"Does anyone? I'm told you telephoned me."

"I did. I'd like to speak with you. About Cheryl Pitman. I'm told you gave some rather surprising information to the police about the recent events in Mrs. Pitman's life."

Aha. So they had decided to act on what she had learned from Orville and Mike. She told Mr. Drew he had heard correctly.

"Could we sit down and talk about it, Sister? Could you by any chance come to my office?"

Kim could hardly refuse to cooperate, after having insisted to Richard that what those two gunmen had told her should be investigated. Not to do so would be to concede that people like Cheryl Pitman were outside or above the law, not subject to the same constraints as the rest of society. Having received instructions from Mr. Drew on how to get there, Kim told him she would be in his office within the hour.

His secretary's name was Winnie Laurel, according to the bronze plate tipped up at an immodest angle to meet the visitor's eye. Her hair was a sprayed cloud of auburn tresses, her eyes sparkled from green eye shadow, her smile had little to do with merriment. It was an uncharitable thought, but Kim could imagine her in a catalogue of office furniture.

"I'm here to see Mr. Drew," she said, keeping a grim face to see if she could defrost that awful smile. "Kimberly Moriarity."

"The nun?" Her surprise was genuine. The smile wavered and for a moment Kim hoped the make-up might run and the hair wilt and fall, certain there was a genuine person lurking behind this cosmetic mask. "*Sister* Kimberly?"

"That's right. Mr. Drew is expecting me."

"Not quite," she said, but then she got her fixed expression of mindless merriment back. "I'll announce you."

Her hand drifted out to the phone, but she thought better of it. She decided to announce Kim in person, perhaps to dispel from Mr. Drew's mind the thought that a nun on the order of Sister Mary Teresa had come to see him.

Stanley Drew was affable and unsurprised and struck Kim as a man without self-doubt. He came to the door, ushered her into the room, got her seated across from his desk, and, when he himself was seated, asked if she minded if he smoked. As he asked, he displayed a beautifully shaped brier pipe. The room was already redolent of pipesmoke. Kim shook her head. While he lit the pipe, he studied her through the flame of a match that leaped in rhythm to his puffing as a cloud of smoke formed around him. By the time he blew out the match, Kim felt he was convinced he knew all he need know about her.

"You told the police Mrs. Cheryl Pitman hired some professional gunmen to shoot at her."

Kim nodded. "Twice. Once while she was staying with

us on Walton Street, again when she was being provided a refuge in our place in Michigan."

"Why would she do a thing like that?"

"I've thought about that. I don't know. It doesn't matter. She hired these men to fake an attempt on her life."

"Fake?"

"That's right. On both occasions there was a great deal of damage and noise, but Cheryl Pitman was never in danger."

"And how did she make her whereabouts known? As I understand it, she was taken in secrecy to the house on Walton and in equal secrecy to this farm in Michigan. How could she have gotten word to her assailants as to where she was?"

"That's a problem whether or not she hired them, isn't it?"

"How do you mean?"

"Twice she was fired on when she was supposedly in houses no one knew of. I should think that is more difficult to explain if she didn't hire them than if she did."

From the outset Kim was conscious of the skepticism of his manner. Her expectation that she would be speaking with a public official eager to act on the information she had received from Orville and Mike had been seeping away as she looked across the desk into the cold and unreceptive eyes of Stanley Drew.

"You don't believe me."

He thought about that. "Tell me the circumstances in which Orville Rollins and . . . " He consulted the yellow pad on which he had been making desultory notes. " . . . Michael Skinner made this extraordinary admission to you."

She told him. She explained that their concern was to enlist her testimony that they could not have been involved in the incident featuring Miriam Pitman. Drew was distracted by the pipe. Indeed, Kim began to wonder if he was listening to her at all. Her temper flared.

"Am I boring you?"

His eyebrows lifted. "Go on. Go on."

"I have the feeling you don't put much credence in what I'm saying."

"It is a rather fanciful tale, don't you agree?"

"It is not a fanciful tale, Mr. Drew. It is the simple truth."

"Please. Don't misunderstand. I don't doubt that you are giving me a perfectly accurate account of what these two men told you. It is their narrative that I call a fanciful tale. Am I right in supposing you have not had much experience with hired gunmen?"

She was being patronized. His tone was openly condescending now. Kim was cast in the role of the naive nun who had taken as gospel truth the tall story of self-confessed felons. She sat in silence for some moments, gaining control over her breathing. To run out of breath while speaking with Mr. Drew would doubtless provide him with an excuse to add hysteria to her other faults.

She said, "Why did you want to see me if you don't believe a word I say?"

"To advise you." He sat forward. "Sister, it is unwise to spread such a story as this about someone like Mrs. Pitman." He looked sad. "It does not befit your calling."

"You think I am slandering her?"

"Let's call it libel."

"Let's not. First, I am not spreading this story about. I told the police. Second, the story is true. A true story told to those with a right to know cannot be characterized as either slander or libel. Third, even if your supposition were right—and I do not think it is—what those gunmen said should be investigated to determine whether it is true or false."

"But that would entail the assumption that Mrs. Pitman is guilty. I need not remind you, that in our legal system . . ."

"You are presuming I am guilty of slander! For

heaven's sake, think of the situations Cheryl Pitman has been involved in during the past two days. Surely, what those men told me casts light on those events."

"May I repeat my advice? Consider whatever duty you had in the matter to have been fulfilled when you told the police. Don't pass it on to anyone else."

"Meaning that you don't intend to pursue it?"

"It will be our secret."

As if to prove the world is not governed by chance, at that moment his phone rang. It was some satisfaction to see the smugness and self-assurance drain from his face while he listened. He glared at Kim as if she had something to do with this favorable alteration in his personality. And she did.

"Bring it in," he growled.

The door opened and Winnie Laurel brought in a copy of the *Tribune*. The story was on the front page, under Katherine Senski's by-line. Heiress Accused of Hiring Assault on Herself and Daughter. Stanley Drew read the account like a prize pupil of speed reading. His expression was venomous when he looked up at Kim. She had stood to spell out the headline upside down and to see Katherine Senski's name beneath it.

"You might have told me you had already been to the newspapers."

"The *Tribune* is not as timid as you, apparently."

"I predict she'll sue you," he said coldly.

As Kim went downstairs in the elevator, she thought, they'll have to sue Sister Mary Teresa too. Kim hadn't talked with Katherine Senski, but she thought she knew who had. It was the sort of thing Emtee Dempsey would do without batting an eye, making sure that what Kim had learned from Orville and Mike would not be buried in official caution and timidity. It was one of the first things she had said when Kim had told her what the gunmen had told her.

"You told only Richard?"

"He's in charge."

"Did he tell you how reluctant he thought the city or state would be to prosecute Mr. Pitman if he were behind those shootings? They will be equally reluctant to bring any charges against her."

At the time Kim had thought these fears unfounded. By the same token, she did not expect action to be taken simply on what she had said or on what the two men had said. She assumed that an investigation would be ordered and that conclusive evidence of Cheryl Pitman's implication in the shootings would be discovered. With such evidence, how could there fail to be a prosecution?

Going home in the Volkswagen Bug, she was no longer so sure. Drew's attitude showed her how unlikely it was that an investigation would be ordered. Now she could believe that if evidence fell into the prosecutor's lap, he would still do anything except act on it. What a depressing thought, and how worse than depressing for Richard. Is justice done if all are not subject to the same standards? How could Richard feel zeal for the apprehension of some wrongdoers if he knew others were simply overlooked, deliberately overlooked, not because their misdeeds were minor, but because they themselves were major figures in society? Kim felt a new sympathy with him. How would he react to the story in the *Trib?*

"What a damned fool thing to do, Kim," Richard said over the phone. "If there was any chance to get her, you blew it when you went to the newspapers. They'll turn her into a martyr."

"No, Richard. You're wrong. She already tried that. Remember the shootings."

"Sometimes I wished they hadn't missed."

"Richard!"

"You know what I mean."

Kim did, but she couldn't admit it to him. She didn't want to scandalize her own brother.

She said, "I'm glad they missed Miriam."

Seven

The big news the next day was that Cheryl Pitman, far from being indignant at Kim for the story that, having first appeared in the *Tribune,* now spread to the other Chicago papers, was demanding the police pick up Orville and Mike and put an end to these ugly rumors so her own safety could be assured. She was joined in her demands by Amos Pitman, once her estranged, now apparently her reconciled, husband. The two of them looked out from the TV screen, their expressions those of hungerers after justice.

"As we understand the story," Amos Pitman said, "these gunmen admit to having fired on my wife twice. Here is certainly a crime. Surely there is no need, there should be no need, to urge the police to perform their duty. A crime has been committed. Two men have admitted committing it. The police have no choice but to bend their better efforts to apprehend these men."

His face remained passive throughout this argument. Kim could imagine him entrancing juries, persuading the naive, consigning to punishment those who had committed no crimes. And she recognized him. Amos Pitman was the man who had been in Jane Corydon's office when Kim was leaving Birnam School after talking with Miriam. Her antipathy wavered at the thought that he showed more parental concern for Miriam than Cheryl Pitman, finding time in a doubtless busy day to visit her school.

Cheryl said, "Charges have been made against me. By self-confessed gunmen. I want to confront these men face to face and see what they will then be able to say. I have been shot at. Twice!" Her voice broke and Amos put an arm around her, hugging her to him.

"Isn't it true a nun brought these charges to the police?" the reporter asked.

Cheryl's weeping was the only answer. The announcer consulted his notes.

"Sister Kimberly Morrison spoke to the gunmen and received their charge that . . ."

Kim permitted the voices to drift away. Morrison! To be wrongly identified seemed to add to the unreality. Could any couple in a similar situation have gone on TV and made a case for themselves as the Pitmans had just done? Kim doubted it. The channel on which it appeared, she recalled, was, if Richard was right, owned by Cheryl Pitman.

"Cheryl Pitman is an amazing person," Sister Mary Teresa said beside Kim.

"She is a liar," Joyce cried, then looked at Kim. "Isn't she?"

"Yes."

"What is she after?" Sister Mary Teresa murmured. "What on earth is she after?"

That remained the real question and it introduced a surd element into everything that had happened. The lawyer's question, Sister Mary Teresa had taught Kim, is *cui bono?* Who profits or gains from what has been done? The question introduces a note of intelligibility into what might otherwise be irrational occurrences. If something is to someone's advantage, that someone has a motive to bring it about. This consideration, more than opportunity, more than circumstantial evidence, is the decisive one. So Sister Mary Teresa had always insisted. But to put that question to the events centering around Cheryl Pitman was to introduce, not dispel, a surd element. Who in the world benefited from the shootings? How could it be said that Cheryl Pitman herself did?

For notoriety? To make someone else look guilty? Richard had suggested that in order to divorce Amos Pitman in such a way that he would have no claim on her wealth, she had only to create the grounded suspicion that he tried to take her life. The difficulty with this theory, as Richard himself had said, was that no state's attorney or district attorney would take on such a case unless he was dragged kicking and screaming into a courtroom where he must face platoons of the best legal aid money could buy. Two other things stood against this theory. One, rather than being driven apart, Cheryl and Amos seemed to have been drawn back together by the recent series of events. Second, there was the apparent assault on Miriam.

It was one thing, in her absence and in the abstract, to imagine Cheryl paying men to feign an assault on her daughter that had put her in real jeopardy of her life; it was something else to believe it in the cool light of a Chicago April morning. Kim found she did not think Cheryl Pitman capable of so low a deed. She studied her face on the TV screen. Cheryl's tears were genuine, her indignation convincing. Grant her at least half. She had, as Orville and Michael had all but admitted, paid for a make-believe assault on herself. But someone else could have repeated the deed with Miriam as the target.

"It is those who injured Miriam I want to see arrested," Emtee Dempsey said. She spoke as if she and the child had been friends for years. Kim said as much.

"Thanks to the vividness and the thoroughness of your

report, Sister, I have a very lively mental picture of the girl."

"Then who would shoot at her?"

"I don't know."

"*Cui bono?*" Kim asked.

"Yes," Sister Mary Teresa growled.

There was one possible motive for Cheryl Pitman, one difficult to grasp, perhaps impossible to understand. Suicide by a hired hand. A longing for a supposed nothingness, surcease of sorrow and of dissatisfying joy too, a metaphysical thirst not to be. Kim could not begin to understand such a thing, but clearly every day, all over the world, human beings sped themselves into eternity by methods ranging from the crude to the most sophisticated. People wanted nothingness. But how can you *be* nothing? This made it a verbal issue and that is not what it was for suicides. Kim had often thought that, up to the last moment, they did not really believe they were going to die, that no matter what harm they had done to themselves, they expected help would arrive in the nick of time and they would be saved.

That could certainly apply to Cheryl Pitman. How calculated and unreal to hire men to shoot at her. That was something she might do while at the same time doubt that such a thing could really be done. The men were paid to miss, but there would be the dreadful and fascinating possibility that one of the bullets would strike her down. The decadent quest for sensation, once confined to the very few, to despots and satraps, was now within reach of an ever-widening circle of people, and Cheryl Pitman certainly fell within that circle.

In any case, it amounted to a strange situation: the police and state's attorney refusing to investigate the charges Kim had made based on the statements of Orville and Mike, their reluctance explained by an unwillingness to cause trouble for people as powerful as Cheryl and her husband; but that same Cheryl and husband insisting the police investigate these charges against her. If Kim were not so far from the ideal of perfection that Blessed Abigail Keineswegs put before her spiritual daughters, she might have felt some sympathy for Stanley Drew. And Richard. Richard was not amused by the plight he found himself in.

"Naturally she claims an investigation would prove her innocent."

"Don't you think it would?" Kim asked.

The sound of his breathing over the phone magnified. "Who knows? We can't find Rollins and Skinner."

"How about the one who shot at Miriam?"

"We want Rollins and Skinner."

"Does Cheryl Pitman know this?"

It was not often that Kim heard obscenities. By the time she realized what Richard had said, he had hung up.

What would he have said if he knew Orville Rollins and Mike Skinner were ensconced in the basement of the house on Walton Street?

"We can offer you sanctuary," Sister Mary Teresa had said when the two men showed up at the house. Kim had taken them into Emptee Dempsey's study. This was something to be decided by her.

"Not in the chapel, Sister," Orville protested.

Sister Mary Teresa looked at Kim, but no one would have guessed she was on the verge of laughter. "Very well. In the basement. Would you take them down there, Sister?"

"Basement" was not quite the word for it, since there was a game room, and another room that elsewhere might have been called a family room, as well as a small apartment that had once been occupied by a maid, before their coming.

"I don't like it," Orville said.

"We gotta be able to see. We gotta have a way out," Mike explained.

"But not the chapel," Orville repeated.

Kim took them into the little apartment. From the bedroom window, through a grill, one could look out on Walton

Street. The two men relaxed. Orville brought out a pint of whiskey, looked sheepishly at Kim, and asked if she minded. She told them to go ahead. In fact, she fetched glasses for them from the kitchen, glasses cloudy with dust before she rinsed them off. The water that came from the faucet in the kitchen sink was rusty at first, but soon it and the glasses were clean. Orville and Mike lifted their glasses in a toast and Kim said they were happy to be able to offer them asylum. They didn't like that word any better than they had "sanctuary." And then Kim asked them why they had sought a refuge.

"Refuge. Yeah," Orville said. "The newspaper story. That's going to get us snuffed if we don't watch out. Why did you have to go tell all that to the paper?"

"It's too late now to do anything about it." What was the point of telling them it was Sister Mary Teresa who had given the story to Katherine Senski? "Have you been threatened?"

They exchanged an impassive look. It seemed better not to pursue it. Clearly they had not come to Walton Street without cause. Perhaps it was only their sense of what entailed what. The newspaper story portrayed them as disclaiming in a panicked way any connection with the attack on little Miriam, and the implication was that they knew who her assailants had been. The surest way to distract attention from themselves would be to focus it on the real culprits. Not that Kim believed they would tell who the others had been. A moral code composed of terror and honor governed their lives.

In any case, she left them with their whiskey and a small television set that began to bring to them the tortured tale of life in the sudsy suburbs.

A half hour later Cheryl Pitman came to the house on Walton Street. Joyce put her in the living room and tiptoed up to get Kim. "Emtee Dempsey doesn't know she's here."

"What does she want?" Joyce's tone made Kim apprehensive. The truth was she didn't relish the thought of confronting the woman she had in effect accused by repeating Orville's and Mike's charges.

"Does she know I'm here?"

Joyce snapped her fingers silently. "I always forget to lie."

"It wouldn't have been a lie," Kim said primly, and recognized Emtee Dempsey's tone in her voice. "I'll go down."

"I am calling on you personally to ask you to aid the police in tracking down those men who made that awful accusation against me."

Cheryl Pitman said these words, standing in the middle of the living room, her large purse clasped in both hands.

"I believed them."

A medium-long silence. Kim could have measured it on the second hand of her watch. "Yes. You're wrong."

"Cheryl, please."

"Look, Sister." She emphasized the word, as if it could be used against Kim. "Whatever you think, whatever I claim, the truth cannot be known until those men are brought in and questioned. Even if you're right and I am lying, the police can only learn who attacked Miriam if they talk with those men."

"Perhaps. But they know about Rollins and Skinner. If having names helps, I've already given them the help you ask."

"They could contact you again."

"What for?"

"Sister, these men are killers! They have shot at me, they have shot at my daughter. What makes you think they would hesitate to shoot at you? You're the one who splashed their names across the front pages of the newspapers. They will be in trouble with their own kind."

"Not to mention with their employer."

Cheryl stalked out. Kim did not really blame her. After closing the door, she went to the study and told Emtee Dempsey Cheryl Pitman had been there.

"I am not surprised. How is her daughter?"

"She didn't say."

"You must visit Miriam again."

"I intend to."

"Good. That is a side of things still obscure to me—the daughter, the mother." She inhaled, puffed her cheeks, expelled air snortingly through her nose. "The husband. The uncle."

Did she mean Cheryl's uncle or Miriam's? She could have meant either. Perusal of the material Katherine Senski had given them provided at least a journalistic view of three people who must be regarded as interested parties: Amos Pitman, Cheryl's husband, and Herbert Stein, her brother, and her uncle, her mother's brother, Franklin. In going through the clippings, Kim had—a student's habit—made résumés, coming up with the following sketches.

"Amos Pitman, born 1931, Chicago, various public schools, then two years at what is now known as Illinois Tech. Before he received his degree, he was deep in the commodity market. By the age of thirty he was a one-man conglomerate with a suite of offices in the Merchandise Mart. Belatedly, it had occurred to him that there were other things in life besides making money, and at the age of forty he began to devote himself to social life with the same tenacity he had to business. He sailed, he took parties to the Indianapolis 500 in a rented railway car, he golfed. And he became a philanthropist. That was how he met Cheryl. When they married it was the first time for him, the second for her. It had not been the kind of marriage he expected, scarcely more than a liaison, and there had been disagreeableness from the beginning."

"What was his model of marriage?" Sister Mary Teresa asked. "What of his family?"

The newspaper accounts in which he figured were silent on that, though the obituary Katherine Senski included did refer to Amos's antecedents. That is, it gave their names. Amos had been an only son. Katherine Senski checked for Kim; both the parents were dead. This exiguous profile (Sister Mary Teresa's description) took on some life for Kim when she saw Amos on television and a great deal more when she spoke to him face to face.

Uncle Franklin, the brother of Cheryl's mother, was, if an interested party, an infrequent presence in Chicago. A graduate of the University of Chicago, seven years older than Cheryl, he had drifted into graduate school with an idea of studying art history; that had led to European trips, inevitably to Florence, a visit had become exile; the ideal of Bernard Berenson and I Tatti had captured Franklin's imagination. Alas, he had little more than this derivative ambition, accompanied by neither insight nor the knack of creating interest in a work where no interest had been before. Nonetheless, he bought a farm in Tuscany where he was said to paint, to make pottery, and do some sculpturing with a welding torch. He had never married, but a succession of coeds and female graduate students had spent extended periods on the farm, their tenure usually interrupted when they began to presume on their closeness to Franklin. One or two disgruntled ones had made public comments on the artwork produced by Franklin, unflattering comments. Few others had been permitted to see his work. As far as Kim could ascertain, Franklin had not been back to Chicago in over ten years.

Herbert Stein was a surprise. There was extremely little on him. The one feature story had been occasioned by the opening of his health food store in Old Town. He glared into a camera, a hirsute man who seemed to be making up for the thinning hair on top with a luxuriant beard. He wore what looked to be a leather vest that exposed his hairy chest and arms. Herbert had the expression and used the rhetoric of one who had turned his face from the world his upbringing had prepared him for (three eastern prep schools, a semester at Yale, a four-year enlistment in the army with service in Vietnam). For wealth and luxury he had exchanged simplicity, though there was no mention of a repudiation of his inheritance; for the skill in killing he had practiced in the jungles of southeast Asia he had traded work with kids in settlement houses in the neighborhood. Miriam said he was the only relative she really liked.

"I would like him even if he weren't my uncle," Miriam said to Kim at the hospital.

"You never mentioned him to me."

"The time you came to Birnam School? But there are lots of things I didn't tell you then. I didn't mention Uncle Franklin either."

"Do you ever see him?"

She shook her head. "No. But he's not Herbert. Herbert is mine. I didn't want him thought of as . . ." She stopped. Had she meant to preserve Herbert from being thought of as in the same group as her mother, her stepfather?

"Do you see Herbert often?"

"Not as often as I like."

This was a sentiment apparently shared by Jane Corydon. The headmistress came to see Miriam while Kim was there at the hospital. A nurse was in the room too and looked up curiously when Miriam greeted her visitor as Dr. Corydon.

"Not a medical doctor," Jane Corydon glossed, but the nurse, having assured herself that whatever authority this erect self satisfied woman might have did not encompass her own activities, ignored the explanation. "Miss Moriarity," Jane Corydon said to Kim.

"Sister Moriarity," Miriam corrected, and she sounded pleased by the thought that she could thus correct the headmistress.

"So I read in the paper," Dr. Corydon said. She had stepped to the side of the bed, put a small package on the table beside it, and laid a gloved hand in frosty benediction on Miriam's head. "I also refreshed my memory on *Doctor* Dempsey."

"Refreshed your memory?"

"I simply did not make the connection. I should have. Particularly considering the circumstances of your visit."

"I don't understand."

"Please." Dr. Corydon gave Kim a no-nonsense smile. "The attack on Mrs. Pitman. It is the sort of meaningless deed that would attract the redoubtable Sister Mary Teresa. And her champion on the *Tribune*."

"You mean Katherine Senski. Why do you say meaningless?"

"I mean unexplained."

"They're not quite synonymous."

Kim supposed they might have gone on fencing over Miriam's bed. Jane Corydon brought out a contradictory streak in her she had difficulty repressing. The woman seemed so enormously pleased with herself. Was that part of being a reformed alcoholic? What should have made Jane Corydon a sympathetic figure only added to what Kim found unlikable in her. But Miriam diverted her from these dark thoughts. She told the headmistress they had been discussing Herbert. The transformation in Jane Corydon at the mention of the name was remarkable. The façade of chilly competence gave way to an almost flustered girlishness.

"Discussing Herbert?" Her glance at Kim was unfocused and wild. "What possible interest could Herbert be to a— a *nun*?" She ended in a kind of a squeal.

"You mustn't worry," Miriam said. "Kim can't get married. She's not interested in men."

Jane Corydon flushed red at this insolent remark. Kim, too, was annoyed. Modern culture is such that the vow of chastity is no longer understood. Obviously—at least it was obvious in another age—unless a matrimony is good and desirable, it makes no sense to regard denying oneself its consolations as a very special gift to God. Nowadays the choice of virginity is likely to be interpreted as due to frigidity or to homosexuality or God knows what. In other circumstances, Kim might have tried to enable Miriam to get some glimmer of the reason for her vow by appealing to stories of women who, having lost the love of their lives, resolved to live out their lives alone. Miss Havisham, "A Rose for Emily," that sort of thing, the romantic springboard from which one might be able to make the leap into a religious resolution to serve God indiscriminately in all rather than specially in one. Kim's consternation at what Miriam had said dulled her perception, and she failed then to appreciate the significance of Miriam's teasing of Jane Corydon.

"She has a crush on Herbert," Miriam explained, after the headmistress had left. Kim had the fugitive thought that Miriam might equally have said Amos. The ten minutes Dr. Corydon had spent in the room were heavy with the sense of duty; having recovered from the flustered reaction to the mention of Uncle Herbert, she had regained her glacial aloofness and spoke of Miriam's classmates. She had refused permission for them to come to the hospital and form beneath the window so Miriam could look out at them. It seemed an extravagance to rent a bus for so distant a salute. Miriam was to stand by for a class phone call that evening. Dr. Corydon had given the class permission to put through a group call. Kim suggested it must be an annoyance to Dr. Corydon to supervise all these activities.

"Not at all. It is my career." Her shoulders went back as she said it.

"Wouldn't it be easier to let Miriam's friends phone her?"

"We do not encourage the use of the telephone at Birnam School. Girls that age would do nothing but hang on the phone if they were permitted private phones. Their access to the school phone must be regulated or they would do the same with it. The discipline is desirable."

"And it lets you know who calls us."

Dr. Corydon smiled, stretching her lips, showing no teeth. "That is scarcely a matter of much intrinsic interest, Miriam. But it is a protection for the girls." Jane Corydon turned to Kim. "Obscene phone calls. You would not believe the things that come to our switchboard."

"Like what?" Miriam sat forward and hugged her knees.

"Never mind. The point is to protect you girls from such filth, not to pass it on to you."

Why did the practices of the school, of which, by and large, Kim approved, sound so fussy and silly as described by Jane Corydon? It was this prim, chilly façade that Kim thought of when Miriam made the surprising remark.

"How can she have a crush on your uncle?" Kim asked. "Does she know him?"

"I told you he comes to see me. At least he did. I think Jane scared him away."

"Hmmm." The sound Kim made was meant to be neutral, lest she seem to be prodding Miriam to gossip, but Miriam reacted as if she were giving her the pitch on which to sing her heart out. Miriam was both angry and amused that someone like Jane Corydon should think she might attract Uncle Herbert.

But beyond her incredulity that Jane Corydon might aspire to win the heart of her uncle, it was her enthralled picture of a free spirit so different from her mother, so indifferent to the things she took seriously, living exactly the life he wanted to live, that fascinated Kim.

"Has he come to see you here?" Kim could not resist the question. If her mother lost credit for coming so infrequently, how could her uncle be her hero if he had not come at all?

"I told him not to."

"Why?"

"I don't want him to see me lying here like a *nudzh*." She looked away as she said it and Kim guessed Uncle Herbert had disappointed her too.

"Has he telephoned?"

"I talk to him on the phone once a day," Miriam said sharply, and Kim imagined her dialing his number, an expectant look on her face. What grounds did she have for such fanciful constructions? Nothing except that they seemed to fit in with Miriam's life as she knew it. Perhaps, subconsciously, Kim wanted some hypothesis to test when she went to visit Herbert.

Mother Earth's Dirty Diets was a storefront, the windows of which had been painted over in a psychedelic riot of primary colors, the crazy palette-like effect relieved here and there by small signs announcing items on sale. Wheat germ was offered at some apparently attractive price, sunflower seeds went for a bird song, and other more exotic items sought to charm the eye of the passerby. Kim had long since decided to leave her diet in Joyce's competent hands and, spoiled by her culinary skills, she had been unable to develop even a theoretical curiosity in such wares as Herbert traded in.

Inside, the clean assault of smells caused her to stop under the tinkling bell that hung above the door. She was re minded of an old-fashioned neighborhood grocery, one of which had persisted near the Moriarity house far into the age of the supermarket, the couple who ran it willing to see their business dwindle to the status of a hobby as long as they could remain among people they knew. Mother Earth's Dirty Diets catered to a somewhat different clientele than had the neighborhood grocery. Kim had not realized there were still men who wore their hair long and women who favored granny gowns, but just such a couple pushed a diminutive shopping cart among the tables, she with a baby strapped papoose-like on her back. In the rear of the store, seated at a desk out of Dickens, his moccasined feet hooked in the rungs of a high stool, was Herbert. He seemed to be wearing the same outfit he had been pictured in when the *Tribune* wrote up the opening of his store two years before. Kim was not at all surprised to see the identifying sign on the desk before him: Uncle Herbert.

"I'm Kim Moriarity," she said to him. "I'm a friend of Miriam's."

"Miriam?"

"Your niece."

His eyes were wide and unblinking and, behind the thick lenses of his glasses, seemed to regard Kim from some moral eminence.

"You're a reporter. Please go. I won't speak about it."

"I am not a reporter. I'm a nun."

His eyes seemed to widen more and Kim could sense the surprise of the shoppers. Herbert ran a hand through his beard. He blinked.

"Nun as in sister?"

"That's right. We once ran a college not far from where the Birnam School is."

His eyes rolled out of sight. "Please. Not while I'm fasting." His eyes settled into place like the fruit in a gambling machine. "It is a crime to send Miriam to a place like that. What sort of introduction to life is that hermetically sealed environment? It's the kind of school they packed Cheryl and me off to. My idea would be to put her in school in a neighborhood like this. Have you ever been to Birnam?"

"I stopped by once, that's all."

"And did you meet the redoubtable Jane?"

"Dr. Corydon?"

"The last of the predatory bachelor girls. Believe me, Sister . . ." He looked at her. "Sister what?"

"Moriarity. Kimberly Moriarity."

"What kind of a nun's name is that?"

"Moriarity? Many religious are Irish."

"I meant the Kimberly."

"It's a long story."

"I believe it."

"Miriam tells me Dr. Corydon is a great admirer of yours."

"Of my money, you mean. My imagined money. I have been swindled out of my inheritance by Cheryl and Amos. Like an ass, I accepted him as my financial manager. He managed me right into the poorhouse." And Uncle Herbert laughed. Loudly. Happily. "The nicest thing he could have done to me. So there remains only the principle of the thing, the principal having been frittered away. I want every red cent they stole from me so I can give it away. I can't think of a more painful penalty than making Cheryl and Amos watch while I dispense money as a tree drops leaves in autumn."

"We did that with our money when we sold the college."

"Gave it away?"

"Yes."

"To whom, archdiocesan charities?" Herbert's voice grew heavy with irony.

"I don't know who the recipients were. We didn't ask their names. We literally handed it out."

"Wonderful! You have robbed me of a precedent but excited my admiration. I am surprised that Jane Corydon would admit such a profligate onto the grounds of her school."

"Is it true you're fighting to sell Simon's house?"

If Herbert had seemed to take an almost childish pleasure in telling her of his desire to continue distributing his inheritance, the mention of the house brought a mean, almost manic, gleam to his eye.

"Do you believe that certain places retain a malevolent presence even when the evil people who lived in them are dead? I do. I don't believe much, but I believe that. Simon was an evil man. My father was an evil man. Cheryl isn't much better, to tell the truth. She inherited all their worst characteristics. Having that house destroyed will be a species of exorcism. And it will be destroyed!" He made a fist and brought it down on the surface of his desk. "If it's the last thing I do I'll watch the wrecking ball turn that rotten mansion into dust."

He fell silent, looked furtively at her, tried to smile as if to diminish the impact of what he had said. Kim remembered Katherine's almost joshing account of the struggle between

Cheryl and Herbert and wondered if it were as innocuous as the reporter thought.

"Have you been to see Miriam?" It was difficult to put the question without making it sound like an accusation.

"And run the risk of running into Corydon? She would be lurking almost etymologically in the corridors. She actually phoned here and tried to nag me into going with her. Miriam will understand."

"I wonder. Look, I just came from there. Jane Corydon has come and gone. The coast is clear."

"How's the kid doing?"

"Fine. She is quite a little lady."

"I know. Amazing. Sometimes I wonder if she's illegitimate. I jest, I jest. But it's hard to think of her and of my great-grandfather as belonging to the same race let alone the same family."

"Ah, your great-grandfather."

"Who told you about him?"

"The Chicago newspapers cover your family fairly thoroughly."

"And you seem to have met most of us. Why?"

So Kim told him the story about Richard bringing Cheryl to Walton Street and of the subsequent move to Michigan. While she spoke, Herbert unwound his legs from his stool and stood with his hands in his back pockets, his head tipped to one side, a smile on his face that grew wider as she spoke. He pointed a finger at her.

"Orville and Mike. You're the one." He clapped his forehead with his palm. "I should have put it together. You are the nun who blew the old whistle on Orville and Mike."

"You sound as if you know them."

"Sister, everyone in this neighborhood knows Orville and Mike. Remember 'The Untouchables'? On TV? Let me tell you, Orville and Mike do." Herbert chuckled, shaking his head.

They were interrupted by the couple with the papoose

and Kim stepped back so they could pay for their purchases. Watching Herbert busy himself with his customers, Kim wondered why he found Orville and Mike so mirthful. She did not remember "The Untouchables" on TV.

"Al Capone," Herbert explained when he was free again. "The Twenties. Prohibition. Saint Valentine's day. All of it. Orville and Mike think of themselves as Chicago hoods."

"What are they?"

"Call them free-lance security men. They've worked here and there, in stores, looking for shoplifters. Mike has been a watchman. And they've provided muscle in various nightclubs. Actually, they are really very decent guys. I like them."

"Are they on health food?"

"They've tried. Backsliders. They're carnivores again, I understand. I haven't seen them in weeks."

"Your sister denies hiring them."

"I don't blame her. Ye gods, if she wanted someone to fake an attempt on her life, she would be risking suicide to choose those two."

"Did she know them?"

Herbert shrugged. "How would she know people like that?"

"Through you."

He thought about it. "Possible, but I don't remember it. Although Cheryl is a customer here."

"Will you go visit Miriam?"

"Don't nag."

"Will you?"

"I don't think so."

"But why?"

"It's a long story." A smile rippled his beard as wind might move through grass. "Like your name."

The fact that Katherine Senski came several times to Walton Street during these days when Kim was absent made it clear that things were going on of which Kim was not being told. At least not by Sister Mary Teresa. Joyce had spilled the beans by quoting Katherine's praise of her cooking. She had been direct when she told Kim of Jane Corydon's visit.

"What did she want?"

"Ask Attila, I don't know. But Jane Corydon cooled her heels in the living room for ten minutes before she was called into the study."

It would do the headmistress good to be kept waiting like that, Kim thought, and then was ashamed of herself. When Kim returned from Herbert's, she was sent down to the basement to check on their guests.

"I told them they had to cook for themselves," Joyce said. "They were upstairs prowling about. I don't want them in my kitchen."

"Good for you. They mustn't be extra work."

"Ha. They send me shopping. You wouldn't believe their grocery list."

"Health foods?"

"Right. Whiskey and beer."

They were sprawled unshaven before the TV and the room was littered with the remains of various junk-food containers. Orville lifted a can of beer in a toast when Kim came in and then, seemingly to his own surprise, crushed it in his hand.

"I'm going stir crazy," he growled as beer ran down his arm.

"Think of it as a vacation," Mike said cheerily, though his words were slurred. "Relax and enjoy. What's going on in the outside world, Sister?"

The news was even then showing on the television screen, but perhaps he could not focus on it. Kim drew his attention to the set. He asked when the ball game ended. Orville wanted to know what ball game.

"I just talked to someone who knows you."

Orville tipped his head and stared at her. "Who?"

"Uncle Herbert."

"He's lying. I don't know him."

"He is Cheryl Pitman's brother. He is the proprietor of Mother Earth's Dirty Diets."

Mike said, "Herbert."

"Did you tell him we're here?" Orville asked.

"Of course not."

"Cross your heart and hope to die?"

"Honest Injun."

They apparently decided to believe her. Mike crossed the room to adjust the television and the two of them fell into an argument as to what channel to watch. Kim left them to their debate. Giving those two sanctuary or asylum or whatever may have been a mistake, but at the time it had seemed the right thing to do.

Upstairs, after spending half an hour in the kitchen with Joyce, Kim plunked down in Sister Mary Teresa's book-lined study and stared at her until she broke the old nun's concentration. The ferocious look she turned on Kim did not intimidate her.

"Tell me what's going on," Kim said.

"Sister, the past consists of an infinity of events. If you want a narration of them you will have to find someone with more leisure and omniscience than I have."

"About Cheryl Pitman," Kim persisted, determined not to be deflected by specious arguments.

"You must talk with your brother."

"I know Katherine has been here. Twice. Have *you* talked with Richard?"

Sister Mary Teresa fished forth a small gold watch from a bosom pocket, pressed the stem so that the cover flew open. She began to move it now closer, now farther from her face, squinting dubiously at it. "He should be here now."

A full minute elapsed before the doorbell rang. She

snapped her watch shut and returned it to her pocket. "Would you let him in, Sister?"

Why was she always providing the old nun with occasions to seemingly produce people out of thin air? Richard wore a harassed, distracted look. He scarcely greeted Kim before hurrying down the hall to Emtee Dempsey's study. She hurried right along after him, suddenly fearful that the door would close behind him and she would continue to be kept in the dark about what was happening in this house. When she was in the study, she pulled the door shut behind her. Richard had come to a stop before Sister Mary Teresa's desk.

"I've come to make an arrest, Sister."

She stood and, doing what she could to make her squat figure look erect, tilted her chin.

"What is the charge?"

"Not you." He turned. "I'm supposed to arrest you, Kim. As an accessory."

"Then why did you just march past me and tell Sister Mary Teresa?"

Her voice broke, though why, she did not know. Perhaps the anguish on his face as he spoke, perhaps the catch of fear when she realized he had been sent for her, perhaps to some degree jealousy that he should tell Emtee the bad news before he told her. Richard seemed to suspect only the last.

"She can help," he said. He turned to the still standing figure of Emtee Dempsey. "Sister, tell me. How do I get out of this one? Tell me, how do I not take Kim down and book her?"

Sister Mary Teresa settled slowly into her chair. Her eyes closed and she lowered herself into her inward depths. While she concentrated, Richard and Kim stood before her desk, two school kids in trouble, praying she would find a way out of their difficulty.

Eight

Emtee Dempsey's solution, insofar as she had one, was Mr. Timothy Rush, once the chief legal advisor of their college, now the overseer of the funds remaining from the sale of the place. "Our lawyer," as Sister Mary Teresa preferred to put it, though Joyce and Kim resisted the implication that they had professional men on retainer to look after their worldly interests. At the moment, needless to say, Kim derived great comfort from the fact that Mr. Rush was, indeed, at their beck and call, or at least at Sister Mary Teresa's. When Emtee Dempsey reached him by telephone, she had to spend several minutes convincing him that Kim had not been arrested for violent protesting, perhaps committing arson in the federal building, or some other felony that would be particularly heinous in the conservative outlook Rush shared with Sister Mary Teresa.

"What, precisely, is the charge?" she asked Richard, not muffling the receiver.

"Material witness and complicity after the fact in a crime."

Emtee Dempsey repeated this to Rush. He agreed to meet them downtown. Having hung up the phone, Sister Mary Teresa rose to her feet. "I shall come with you, Sister."

"You will not," Kim said. "I'm perfectly capable of being arrested by myself."

"Nonsense. What are Sisters for?"

"Maybe we should bring Joyce too."

Richard said almost apologetically, "I can't arrest you too, S'ter. I only have a warrant for Kim."

"Joyce can hold the fort," Emtee Dempsey said, and suddenly Kim thought of the men downstairs in the basement apartment. They were her supposed partners in crime, and, if the police knew of their whereabouts, she was sure the warrant for her arrest would have been canceled. For a fleeting moment she felt an impulse to tell Richard they were down there. Actually to be taken away and booked for something she hadn't done seemed so preposterous a thing when telling about those men would restore things quickly to normal. But the temptation was fleeting. There was also the attraction of being arrested. After all, how many nuns have been imprisoned? Even in the headiest days of protests, nuns seemed to be by-passed in favor of male transgressors. And what could be sweeter than to be locked up for something she had not done? She would have the twin goods of innocence and a sense of injury. Besides, think of all the great personages who had produced deathless literature in their cells—Boethius, Socrates . . .

"The Marquis de Sade," Sister Mary Teresa added sourly, when Kim voiced the thought. "I will bring you a notebook on visiting day and you can keep a prison diary."

Richard seemed put at ease by this banter; it helped Kim's own mood considerably. Nor did she long resist Sister Mary Teresa's determination to come along; she doubted she would have been successful if she had.

Kim was booked as a material witness and an accessory

after the fact, the charge being that not only had she conspired with Orville Rollins and Michael Skinner to stage an attack on Cheryl Pitman and her daughter, she had also sought to divert the police by accusing the victim of being her own attacker. Furthermore, she was unwilling to cooperate with the police in their efforts to locate her fellow criminals.

It was the last point that drained her righteous indignation of conviction. She was, after all, a party to concealing the whereabouts of Orville and Michael, but it was safety from others like themselves rather than from the police that was being provided them.

"Utter nonsense," Sister Mary Teresa huffed. "Who has put you up to this?"

The judge, a woman of middle age whose blonde hair hadn't got the message, raised her brows in aristocratic disapproval and sighted through half glasses at the stocky figure in medieval garb who dared address her thus in her own courtroom.

"I'll handle this," Rush said. He was spare and tall and elegant. He wore a dark suit and striped tie and his white hair, not as thick as it must once have been, was arranged in elegant ringlets on his head.

"The charges are brought by the state," Stanley Drew said, his tone one of boredom.

"Is Kimberly Moriarity in court?" the judge asked, her eyes searching a far horizon as if she were on the great plains rather than in her rather modest-sized courtroom.

Rush said, "She is in court."

"Read the charge."

Drew read the charge as if it was only with a great effort that he was keeping sleep at bay. How like an object Kim felt. Championed and protected by Sister Mary Teresa and Rush, though with varying degrees of enthusiasm; an object of accusation by Stanley Drew; a specimen for the judge whose name, it emerged, was Maggie Curran. The fact that Drew had become her accuser restored her sense of injured innocence.

How relieved he must feel to have effected a unification of his supposed duty and an opportunity to be of service to Cheryl and Amos Pitman.

"How do you plead?"

Judge Curran addressed Kim, but, of course, it was Rush who answered.

"Not guilty. Your Honor, with all respect, I must concur with the opinion expressed by the good lady to my left. These charges are utter nonsense. Kimberly Moriarity, like Mary Teresa Dempsey, is a religious of the Order of Martha and Mary and . . ."

"A nun!"

"A nun, Your Honor."

Maggie Curran sat forward. She looked sharply at Stanley Drew, then leaned farther forward to get a better look at Kim. "You are Sister Kimberly Moriarity?"

"Yes." Her voice sounded remote. She cleared her throat and repeated, "Yes."

"And the nun seated there is a member of the same order as you?"

"This is Sister Mary Teresa Dempsey," Kim said.

"Aha." Again the judge looked sharply at Drew. "I am delighted to have you in my court, Sister Mary Teresa," Maggie Curran said with some unction.

"I plead innocent too, " Emtee Dempsey said. Drew chuckled in a good sportsman's way and Maggie Curran beamed.

"You no longer wear the habit?" the judge asked Kim, and her voice was heavy with disapproval.

"It is optional now."

"Perhaps if you had been wearing it, the events that have brought you here would not have occurred."

"I'm sure of it, Your Honor."

Sister Mary Teresa spoke emphatically. "She is not to be criticized for that, Your Honor. She was on an errand of mercy. She was, as it happens, doing a favor for me. I suppose that by all rights I, too, should be included in this ridiculous indictment."

"With all due respect," Drew said, his chuckle under control, "the charges against Kimberly Moriarity were not brought lightly. Your Honor will know the circumspection and care with which my office operates. We, too, are aware of Sister Moriarity's connection with Sister Mary Teresa Dempsey, and you may be sure such a connection gave us pause when we discussed drawing up this indictment. But just as there cannot be guilt by association, so there cannot be eminence or innocence merely by association."

"Poppycock." Sister Mary Teresa shifted her weight and her rosary clattered against the chair.

Drew ignored this and placed a folder on the judge's desk. Maggie Curran told him to proceed.

Listening, Kim marveled at how a series of events could be so described as to seem heavy with guilty implication. Kimberly Moriarity had been present in the house on Walton Street when the first attack was made on Cheryl Pitman. Kimberly Moriarity had visited Miriam Pitman at her school the following day and under false pretenses. Miriam Pitman herself was soon to be an intended victim. Kimberly Moriarity was present again in the house in Michigan when the second attempt was made on Cheryl Pitman. It was Kimberly Moriarity, furthermore, who had given to the newspapers the preposterous suggestion that Cheryl Pitman had hired Orville Rollins and Michael Skinner to shoot at herself. Doubtless she knew even now the whereabouts of that sought-for couple. And why on earth had she paid a visit on Herbert Stein? Why had she visited Miriam Pitman in the hospital? There was too much to be ignored here, Mr. Drew opined, and he knew Her Honor would agree there was reasonable cause for an indictment. Furthermore, he would suggest that bail not be allowed, given the accused's penchant for scurrying about and precipitating injurious events.

Kim squirmed in her chair, wanting to speak out,

wanting to defend herself. Maggie Curran seemed to ignore Drew while he spoke, busying herself with pad and pencil. When she did look up, she sighted over the heads of those before her.

"I release you in the custody of Sister Mary Teresa."

And with that she rose and swept into her chambers.

Emtee Dempsey took this as vindication enough, but she could not forbear having a word with Stanley Drew before she left the courtroom. As Kim went out with Rush, she could hear scolding tones and she felt fleetingly sorry for Drew. In the corridor, Richard awaited her and the expression on his face would have been appropriate if he were greeting someone who had just been condemned to death. She told him she had been released in Sister Mary Teresa's custody.

"Come here." He took her arm and led her swiftly down the hall. "Something's happened."

"What?"

"Cheryl Pitman had a brother."

"I know. Herbert."

"How do you know about him?"

"Is it a secret? Miriam mentioned him. He was in some of the clippings Katherine Senski gave me." Kim stopped, conscious of the fact that she was sounding apologetic. "What about him?"

"He's dead."

"Dead!"

"Shot. Twice. A very messy sight."

"Dear God. Richard, I just talked with him. He was so vital, so witty."

"When was this?"

"This afternoon. Richard, when did this happen? *Where* did it happen?"

"At his store. He has a health food . . . But I suppose you know all about that."

"Richard, I went to see him because of the way Miriam

spoke of him. He was one relative she really liked. I wanted to ask him to visit her in the hospital. The strangest thing, he knows the men who shot at Cheryl Pitman. Only he doesn't believe they would do such a thing."

"He told you he knew them?"

"Yes. And if he knew them . . ."

Richard made an impatient gesture. "Damn it, Kim. No more theories. Please. Why didn't he think Orville and Mike would be hit men?"

"He thinks they're clowns."

"Look, if he could have identified them, said something about them, testified, you would be a lot better off in fighting the charges against you."

Kim was thinking of her return home to Walton Street after her talk with Herbert. She reconstructed the scene in which she had told Orville and Mike of her visit to the health food store. What if Herbert was wrong about those two men? What if, despite their condition, they had seen Herbert as a further threat to their safety?

"Richard," she said, "I want you to come with me to Walton Street. Do you have a car?"

"Rush will take you and Sister Mary Teresa back there."

"I'd rather we went ahead. Richard, there's something you don't know. Orville Rollins and Mike Skinner have been staying in the basement of our house."

If he had hurried her away from Timothy Rush before, he fairly yanked her down the corridor now, breaking into a run so Kim had to too, and they went loping along with people stepping to the sides of the corridor and looking at them as though they were staging a prison break. As they spun through the revolving doors, Kim had a backward glimpse of Timothy Rush and Sister Mary Teresa standing in the center of the corridor just outside Judge Curran's courtroom, staring after them with enormous disapproval.

❀ *147* ❀

Kim had not often ridden in a police car with full siren and flashing top light, but then, as on the other occasions, she sensed the antinomian freedom that attends the life of the guardians of the law. They sailed through intersections, they hit seventy going along Lake Shore Drive. They did not speak. Richard, grim-faced, was hunched over the wheel. Kim had no inclination to talk. If he had ever wanted to administer physical punishment to her, this was one of the times, and however preferable it was for him to take it out on the police car, Kim began to find the speed and recklessness with which he drove unsettling. When she did speak, it was in a small voice.

"I'm sorry, Richard."

He glared at her briefly. He had turned away and was staring straight ahead when he said it.

"Tell it to Uncle Herbert, Kim."

He stopped the siren before turning into Walton Street and, when he came to a stop across from the house, they might have been just another vehicle taking advantage of a parking space. When Kim had come around the car, Richard took her wrist and then wove expertly through the hurtling traffic to the other side, although Kim's heart was in her throat as she tried to ignore the cars bearing down on them.

At the door, Richard stood next to her, visibly impatient for her to open it and, predictably, she had difficulty getting the key into the lock. Before she did, the light above their heads went on with a suddenness that gave Kim the sensation they had just been photographed. The curtain on the door parted and the startled face of Joyce looked out at them. Beside Kim Richard groaned.

"Nothing like having our arrival announced."

The door opened and Joyce said, "It's you. Did you beat the rap?"

"No, I rang the bell."

Richard pushed past her and as he headed down the hallway to the basement door he drew his revolver from a holster in the small of his back. Kim ran after him aghast at what Orville and Mike might do if Richard burst in upon them with that gun in his hand. Were they armed? Even to ask the question was to recognize how silly it was. Gunmen not armed? Yet she had never given the matter a thought before. If she had, she would have demanded they disarm as a condition of their stay ing with them. Joyce came clattering after her and they went down the stairs after Richard.

"Orville," Kim trilled. "Mike. It's me."

When he reached the bottom of the stairs, Richard stopped and waited for Kim and Joyce to come down. His expression was one of total disgust. He gestured ahead with the gun.

"You go first," he whispered hoarsely.

"That's what I was going to suggest."

"Is that thing loaded?" Joyce asked, staring pop-eyed at Richard's gun.

"I hope so."

Kim proceeded toward the door of the basement apartment, calling out their names again. The door was ajar and she knocked on it playfully as she entered, although the apprehension she had felt on the wild drive from downtown had returned. The television was audible, but when she came into the living room there was no sign of the two men. If she had feared finding them, she was more appalled not to find them. She started toward the bedroom door, but Richard, at her side again, gripped her arm. He shook his head.

"I'll look."

"Be careful."

He opened the door with his foot, lifting it slowly with the grace of a ballet dancer and then kicking with great force. He was through the door almost before it swung open. Joyce had come to a stop in the middle of the living room and now closed her eyes and clamped her hands over her ears. Kim waited too. Joyce's eyes opened questioningly. Kim shook her head. And then Richard reappeared.

"Gone." He looked briefly at Kim. "Not that I'm surprised."

"I didn't hear them leave," Joyce said.

Richard picked up the telephone, put it to his ear, took it away, shook it, tried it again. Kim told him it wasn't hooked up. He put it down.

"What's going on?" Joyce asked.

How Kim envied the innocence that permitted Joyce to ask such a question, and how could she answer it without revealing what a dreadful thing she had done? Her eyes filled with tears and Joyce, looking at her, responded to the grief she manifested. Richard went bounding up the steps and Kim imagined Orville and Mike doing the same when they went off to kill Herbert. She did not even try to stop the tears now and, sobbing, she thought of little Miriam, her beloved uncle dead. And she was responsible. Joyce tried to comfort her, but at the time Kim doubted she could ever again think of herself without a sense of loathing.

Herbert had been alone in his store when he was shot, no one in the neighborhood had noticed anything, or anyone, that might help the police. The police had not expected any help, not in that neighborhood. Herbert was found slumped behind his desk in the back of the store. He had been shot twice, in the chest and in the face. Kim stopped Richard before he went into any details. The murder weapon lay beside the body. A Luger.

"A Luger!"

Richard nodded. "Yes. And it came from Walton Street. They must have grabbed it on their way out. How would they have known there was a Luger in a convent?"

"What possible motive would they have had?" Kim asked, and her voice sounded thin and unreal. "What had Herbert ever done to them?"

"Maybe nothing. Maybe they worried about what he might do."

*　*　*

Sister Mary Teresa, who had scolded Kim for taking responsibility for Herbert's death ("Don't flatter yourself, Sister. Those men have free will. What you told them did not force them to do what they did."), was uncharacteristically reluctant to speculate on the motives of Orville and Michael. Kim's guess that they had acted in the hope of taking pressure off themselves did not convince her.

"The deed is incommensurate. The putative other men are guilty of armed assault. If apprehended, they can fall back on the excuse already provided them. They were hired to frighten, not to kill. That hardly makes them murderers by intent or in fact."

"Maybe not this time."

"*Cui bono?*" Sister Mary Teresa said didactically.

"That's just what I'm telling you. A dead Herbert can't inform on them."

"Surely there are other more substantive advantages that others will enjoy because this man has died."

"He left no will. He refused to draw one up."

"That does not mean he has no heirs."

It was true that Herbert had rejected suggestions of Amos Pitman and of his sister, Cheryl, that he have a will drawn up. Nonetheless, it turned out he had written a will in his own hand. An examination of his safe deposit box, impounded as soon as his death became known, turned up Herbert's last will and testament. He left everything to Miriam. Miriam, released from the hospital, had been taken back to Birnam School, and it was there, with a red-eyed Jane Corydon looking on, that Kim next talked to her.

"I visited his store and talked to him," Kim said.

Jane Corydon glared at her. In the conversation they had had before going in to talk to Miriam, there arose the matter of Orville and Mike staying in the basement apartment on Walton Street—something Katherine Senski had devoted columns to in the *Tribune* (so much for friendship when a newsy item like that was available to her)—and Jane, having suggested the men had forced themselves on them, something Kim had to deny, from being receptive became cool. She had not grasped the full import of Kim's denial before they went to Miriam, and Kim hoped the realization, when it came, would not lead to a scene in front of the child.

"He wouldn't want a funeral, but they don't care. They'll put on a circus."

Miriam spoke in the same dissociated way she had when Kim first met her. Uncle Herbert was dead. There was no one left with whom she could feel identified or akin to. Kim tried to convince her that her mother and stepfather were only showing respect for Herbert by giving him the kind of funeral they planned, but she did not really expect to succeed. Cheryl would have it appear that, like herself, her brother had been part of the social mainstream of Chicago rather than an intentional dropout who had thumbed his nose at her set from his health food store. It turned out they did have that in common, Cheryl and Herbert, a belief in health foods. She had summoned Kim into her presence when the news that Kim had been concealing the gunmen on Walton Street became known. Kim went only because Sister Mary Teresa insisted she go.

In the living room of a very modern apartment filled with antiques, its windows looking out over the lake, Cheryl Pitman served Kim tea and stern advice. The advice was presumptuous, the tea was herbal. Cheryl had been reluctant to pour for Kim, asking if she didn't prefer coffee.

"Tea would be fine."

Still Cheryl hesitated. "It's from my brother's store. I am addicted to it and really rather selfish about sharing it, as Herbert knew. After what I'd just told him, I'm surprised he sent it over. Now that he's dead I wonder if I'll find it easy to be re-supplied."

"What had you told him?"

"It will be announced next week. My great-grandfather's mansion will be declared an historic site. Herbert would have been paid for it and he would have thrown the money away, although I would have tried to stop him."

"What did he say when you told him?"

"He gurgled with rage. He threatened to go ahead and knock the building down before the declaration was public. Of course there was a court order preventing him from doing anything while the matter was being decided." She shook her head sadly. "Poor Herbert. He had none of the family characteristics, the ones that have enabled us . . ." She stopped, constrained by the expression on Kim's face if not by modesty. "And now he is dead," Cheryl said with an odd intonation.

Kim sipped the tea, if only to refrain from answering Cheryl. Alone she might accuse herself of complicity in the killing of Herbert, but to find that accusation present in the manner and tone of Cheryl Pitman made her feel innocent as the driven snow.

Cheryl said, "You actually hid those men in your house?"

"Much as we did you."

"It's hardly the same thing."

"Actually, the two events are intimately connected."

That was when she gave Kim the advice. Stanley Drew had told her how Kim had come to him with the preposterous story those two gunmen had told her. Quite apart from the laws of libel, she knew it was unnecessary to remind Kim of her Christian obligation not to spread scandal or ruin the good name of another. We are all preachers, Kim thought, and never more so than when guilt weighs upon us.

"If their story is true—" she began, but Cheryl interrupted her.

"It is false! You should know that. I did not hire them to shoot at me and my daughter. Good heavens, will you think about that ? Does the story make any sense at all to you?"

"No, it doesn't," Kim said.

"Still you believe it?"

"What kind of tea is this?"

She decided to allow Kim to deflect her from the topic as to which of them was more responsible for her brother's death. The tea was a powdery mixture, still in the brown bag she had received it in, though she kept that in a canister on her tea cart. Kim did not like the taste of it and drank it out of nervousness rather than politeness.

That had been the day before her visit to Miriam at Birnam School. For much of the morning she had felt under the weather and would have postponed the visit if she could have rid her mind of the woebegone image of Miriam. Doubtless it was fanciful of her to think a visit from a nun she scarcely knew could make much difference in her day, but they had gotten along so well she felt she could cheer Miriam up or at least make the grief easier to bear. In full command once more of her stoic persona, Miriam was not admitting any grief at all, except indirectly, as in the remark about her parents' plans for Herbert's funeral.

"I'll attend the funeral with you, if you like."

"Can you? It won't be Catholic, you know. It won't be much of anything, from that point of view. We're not a religious family."

She made it sound like not having freckles. There are genetic factors involved in just about any aspect of our lives, Kim supposed, but something like religious belief cannot be accounted for that way. For Kim, it was a profound deprivation for Miriam to have been brought up without a lively sense of God, of her dependence on Him, of His infinite concern and love for her. It may be that there are other than religious ways to make sense of life, but Kim could not imagine them. In these circumstances, it was very difficult for her not to try to convey to Miriam what a religious outlook on life was like, but she was resolved not to do this. Sister Mary Teresa always insisted that the deepest influence is through what we are rather than what we say. If God chose to make use of Kim to catch Miriam's attention, He could do so without a lot of prompting from her.

The service was in the chapel of a funeral home, a chapel that not only sought some least common denominator of the various sects in an ecumenical blandness, but seemed to extend its embrace to unbelievers as well. The only sense of life after death that crept into the proceedings had to do with the continuing memory of Herbert on the part of those there. Cheryl wore black and her mantilla covered her face. After the readings, mainly selections of poetry, but a psalm too, inevitably the Twenty-third, Cheryl and Amos, with a manifestly reluctant Miriam at their sides, received condolences to the right of the now closed casket. Cheryl pinned back her veil, and Kim was struck by her pale and pained countenance.

"I have not been feeling well," she said.

"It is a difficult time," Kim answered.

"Yes. But it's more than that." She shook her head slightly, as if to drive away the thought. An ailing Cheryl Pitman did not match the image she sought to project. "I'm grateful to you for taking such an interest in Miriam."

"That's not a chore."

"She admires you. That's an achievement, if you don't mind my saying so. I mean, because you're a nun. I hope I don't offend you."

"I understand what you mean."

Miriam gave Kim her hand with slightly exaggerated formality. The expression in her eyes invited Kim to see through her pose.

"How good of you to come, Sister."

"Shame on you."

"You know what I mean."

Several people had turned, in curiosity, when they heard the way Miriam addressed her. What would they have made of Sister Mary Teresa if she had chosen to come? To Kim's surprise, she had considered it.

"I would like the chance to see them all together."

"All who?"

"Your reports are vivid and thorough, but I would like to supplement them with a personal inspection."

Kim resisted telling her she would be more inspected than inspecting in such a group. In the end her disinclination to interrupt the schedule that governed her life decided the matter. She had not known Herbert, so it would have been ghoulish to show up at his funeral. But, since his life had impinged however tangentially on hers, he would have a claim on her prayers. He made a claim on her curiosity as well. She had Kim bring home to her an armful of books on health foods, health food stores, so-called natural foods, herbs and the like. When Kim mentioned that various common weeds showed up in the diets of health food faddists, she gave Kim a look.

"Don't be a snob. What is the definition of a weed, I wonder. Why isn't grass one, or oats and barley?"

It was seldom that she sought to shame Kim with such leveling rhetoric; more often than not she was the champion of gradation and hierarchy. Emtee Dempsey as the defender of the common weed was a revelation.

When Kim came to Amos Pitman, he held the hand she extended to him, put his hand on Kim's elbow, and walked her across the room to a corner. On a table before a mirror, a vase of artificial flowers added a dash of color to the bogus room.

"I should be grateful to you for being the occasion of my reconciliation with Cheryl," he said. His gray eyes above the half smile were cold. "I am not. That was not your intention so you will get no credit for it from me."

"I never expected any."

"What you do get is blame. Cheryl, in the shock of Herbert's death, is inclined to forget the libelous statements you made about her. I am not. The fact that you also harbored those criminals, and were doing so at the very time you were urging the state's attorney to bring charges against my wife, magnifies your crime. You are under indictment. I intend to press and press until you are brought to trial and found guilty of the crime you have committed. Your claim to be a religious woman does not impress me. It does not gain you exemption from the law. You have a lesson to learn and I mean to see that you learn it."

These venomous words were spoken with a hatred that was almost palpable and was the more frightening because throughout the threat his smile did not waver. An observer might have thought they were engaged in harmless chitchat. To say Kim was dumfounded by what he said falls far short of expressing the profound sense of vulnerability that came over her. She remembered Richard saying how the state's attorney would not want to run afoul of the ire of the Pitman family. At the time she had felt morally superior to such alleged public servants. Now, feeling the full freezing force of Amos Pitman's vindictive hatred, she wanted to run, to apologize, to beg him not to do what he threatened to do. And yet, to her immense surprise, she could still speak.

"And you will do all this to vindicate your wife?"

"That is much of it, yes."

"But what if it's true? What if she did hire those men?"

His smile broadened and he squeezed her elbow painfully. "The point is it's false. She didn't hire them. And you know it."

He let go of her elbow and turned. Kim watched him go back across the room and she saw, too, that Miriam was staring at her. She had the sudden certainty that Miriam had watched, and alone of those in the room was undeceived by Amos Pitman's smile as he spoke to her. Miriam came toward her, passing her stepfather without a glance at him.

"What did he say?"

"He is angry with me."

"Because of the hired gunmen story?"

"Is that what you think it is, a story?"

Miriam looked at her a moment, as if wishing not to hurt her feelings. "My mother wouldn't know a gunman if he was robbing her. Even if she did, she would never ask them to do what happened."

"Oh, Miriam, I know she had no intention of your being harmed."

"I meant, she would never have them shoot at herself. That would be too risky. Besides, there are lots of easier ways of getting rid of Amos."

"You think that would have been the reason?"

"I know she wanted to get rid of him. And probably vice versa. Oh." Miriam had seen something behind Kim that caused her mouth to drop open. Kim turned and saw Jane Corydon standing in the doorway of the chapel. Her arms hung limply at her sides, her shoulders were hunched forward, her face was twisted in horror as she stared at the closed casket containing the body of Herbert. If she saw anyone else, she gave no sign of it. And then she began to move slowly across the room toward the casket while her expression became, if possible, more tortured. A hush had fallen over the room and there was an air of expectancy, as if they all awaited something dreadful to happen. It seemed they all knew she had loved Herbert. Cheryl, perhaps involuntarily, took a step backward as Jane Corydon started across the room. Amos frowned, but stepped back with her. It was Miriam who instinctively did the right thing.

In several swift steps she reached Jane Corydon's side and, taking her hand, continued walking with her headmistress toward the closed coffin. If Jane Corydon noticed Miriam, it did not slow her progress to the casket. They stopped a step or two before they reached it. From where Kim stood she could no longer see Jane Corydon's face, but then her slumped shoulders heaved and the sound of her sobbing filled the room. It was the only weeping that had been done for Herbert.

Cheryl was horrified by the sound of uncontrolled crying. Looping her arm through Amos's, she hastened out of the chapel, pulling with her the vast bulk of the mourners. "Tell them to get that woman out of here," she hissed at Amos. "I do not want her making a spectacle of herself at the cemetery."

But it was Miriam who made certain Jane Corydon was given space in one of the limousines with which the funeral director conveyed favored guests as well as the immediate family to the burial site. Kim rode in the same car. At Miriam's insistence. After Amos had threatened her, she wanted nothing more than to get away from this family in which the currents of passion swirled so unpredictably. But how could she refuse Miriam's insistence that she come with her? Miriam's eyes darted sideways to Jane Corydon, in an appeal for Kim's help with the grief-stricken headmistress. Jane Corydon herself looked at Kim with red-rimmed eyes as if she was not sure who she was. No wonder. Once in the car, the unmistakable smell of liquor emerged on Jane Corydon's sobs. Perhaps she would have fitted right in at an Irish wake, but her condition was not calculated to commend her to this crowd.

"I wanted to get there before they closed the coffin."

"No, you didn't," Miriam said. "It wasn't Uncle Herbert. It was just a thing."

This was not calculated to console Jane Corydon, but then nothing could have, with her genuine sorrow enhanced by the amount she had drunk. There is a pleasure to be taken from mourning, a self-referential pleasure, and maybe, if one does not think the deceased in any way still exists, this is less wrong than it would be otherwise. On the way to the cemetery, Jane Corydon confided to the world that she and Herbert had talked of marriage, though she went into no details as to what the upshot of the conversation had been. In any case, she apparently wanted to cast herself in the moral equivalent of the widow's role.

When they arrived at the cemetery, when they had been driven slowly up the narrow avenues over which burgeoning trees brooded in a metaphor of melancholy, and had come to a stop with the other limousines, two of the funeral director's men came to the car and, after Miriam and Kim had descended, replaced them on either side of Jane Corydon. They pulled the doors closed after themselves. Miriam protested and grabbed the handle, but not before Jane Corydon had locked the door from within.

"Come, Miriam," Kim said. "It's really for the best."

"At least she cried." And, after they had walked some distance from the car, "I wish I could."

But it was Cheryl Pitman herself who provided what dramatics remained. At graveside, the director read some Tennyson and, when he had finished, Cheryl slumped against Amos, clutching her side. He tried to help her to an erect position, but she shook her head and leaned forward. A moan escaped her. Did some fugitive memory of her brother when they were young and innocent suddenly overwhelm her? Amos Pitman, looking concerned and embarrassed, helped her back across the lawn to the waiting car.

No one was more surprised than Miriam. She watched her mother's halting, supported progress and in her now moist eyes there was a wondering, almost loving look.

Nine

After the funeral, it had fallen to Kim, she was not quite sure why, to look after Jane Corydon. The headmistress was in no condition to look after herself, and there certainly could be no question of her continuing to make a nuisance of herself with the mourners. Amos Pitman, when he came to take Miriam away, asked Kim to do something about Jane Corydon.

"Before she makes a complete fool of herself." He paused. "She is headmistress of Miriam's school."

"I know."

"I suppose that's how she got to know Herbert."

His expression as his gaze met Kim's was brazen. Did he really think she had not seen him in Jane Corydon's office at the Birnam School? Cheryl had said it was Amos who had discovered the school and was instrumental in Miriam's going there. Kim had gotten the impression that both Amos and Cheryl had been impressed by Jane Corydon's victory over alcohol. Now he spoke of the headmistress's knowing Herbert as if it were a conspiratorial deed.

Kim said, "Perhaps she is interested in health foods."

Amos made a face. His expression seemed to dismiss not only the trade Herbert had engaged in but the backsliding headmistress. The headmistress's condition had brought on this pretense that he did not quite know who Jane Corydon was.

Kim left, with Jane Corydon. Miriam came along with the two of them to where Kim had parked the VW in the huge lot behind the funeral home.

"We're going to take a vacation," Miriam said mournfully. "We need to get away." The last was in imitation of her mother, Kim supposed, or it could have been of Amos. Amos Pitman seemed far more in charge now than Kim had ever expected to see him. Even Miriam seemed docile in his regard, a change impossible not to notice. Toward Jane Corydon Miriam behaved now in an almost motherly way. After they had gotten Jane into the car and had closed the door on her, Miriam came around to the other door with Kim and, before Kim opened it, said, "She *loved* Uncle Herbert! Funny, I never suspected she felt as much as that! But she always wanted to talk about him. She even tried to like that awful food Herbert sold."

"She went to his store?"

"Yes." Miriam shook her head. "I'm so dumb. I never thought."

"Did Herbert ever talk about her?"

A pained expression flickered across Miriam's face. She looked at Kim as if pleading for understanding of what she was about to say. "He thought she was, well . . . funny. An old maid. But he did like her, in a way."

It says much of the condition of Jane Corydon that they could stand there and discuss her within feet of her and, who knows, perhaps within earshot as well. But the poor woman was so obviously undone by grief that Kim did not give it a thought. She gave Miriam a hug and slipped in behind the wheel. While Kim started out of the parking lot, Jane's sobs became measured and she seemed to be making an effort to gain control of herself.

"I'm sorry," she said, her voice breaking.

Kim patted her hand. "You and Herbert talked of marriage?"

"Who told you that?" She seemed surprised to hear what she had told Miriam and Kim on the way to the cemetery. Kim reminded her of this.

"Oh, I'm not myself." The smell of liquor was still heavy on her breath and her eyes were dull. Remembering the prim, status-conscious woman she had first met at the Birnam School, Kim wondered which was the real Jane Corydon, the crisp career woman, already in a position of some eminence, or this half-unhinged emotional woman, seemingly as ready as any domesticated matron of yore to see her own life as over, now that the man she had loved was dead.

Kim took her home with her to Walton Street. To have taken her back to the headmistress's apartment on the campus of the Birnam School would have been a disservice; if Miriam had been unaware of Jane Corydon's true feelings toward her Uncle Herbert, Kim rather doubted that any of the other children would have noticed. The drinking, she was convinced, was an uncharacteristic response to a unique event. But it took some persuasion to get Jane into the house when they arrived at Walton Street.

"Where are we?"

"Home. We'll have some coffee and . . ."

Jane leaned forward and looked at the house. "It still doesn't look like a convent."

"It's a house. A home. Surely you're not afraid."

Doubtless fueled by her drinking, Jane Corydon's mind seemed to be full of stories of convent kidnappings, incarcerated maids pressed into the service of the Lord, perhaps a wisp or two of Maria Monk herself. Well, no doubt Kim's head too was filled with crazy little stories about others, stories she knew to be false, but which did not thereby lose all their power to influence judgment.

As luck would have it, as soon as they got inside the door, Sister Mary Teresa came thumping down the hall to greet them in the full panoply of the kind of nun that strikes fear into the uninitiated. Oddly enough, Jane Corydon had no adverse reaction to Emtee Dempsey, the familiar face canceling out her apprehension. But the old nun picked up the scent of drink. Her brows dipped and, leaning on her cane, she peered suspiciously at Jane Corydon and then at Kim.

"I invited Dr. Corydon in for coffee," Kim said, her voice freighted with significance.

"It is a myth that coffee hastens sobriety."

"I'd like some coffee," Jane Corydon said docilely.

Emtee Dempsey squinted at the visitor and shook her head. "Nonsense. Sister Kimberly, bring some liquor from the kitchen. Dr. Corydon and I will be in my study." She said to Jane, "Is that bourbon I smell on you?"

The startled headmistress nodded.

"Bourbon," Emtee Dempsey said, amending her instructions to Kim. She took Jane Corydon's hand and let her off to the study.

Kim did not hesitate. Jane Corydon was taken by surprise and might be excused for permitting herself to be treated like a child by Sister Mary Teresa, but Kim had years of experience and might have been expected to act her own age. Nonetheless, she was in the kitchen before any mutinous thoughts even occurred to her. Joyce turned from the table where she was rolling pie dough.

"How was the funeral?"

"Do we have any bourbon?"

"That bad, huh?"

"We have company. Emtee Dempsey wants to give her a drink."

"Not Cheryl Pitman, I hope."

"No. Jane Corydon. The headmistress of Birnam School, where Miriam Pitman goes. She is already drunk, so I don't know what Emtee Dempsey has in mind."

Joyce put out her lower lip and tipped her head and then opened a cupboard above the refrigerator. She needed to stand on a chair to get the bottle of liquor. "Two glasses or three?" she asked over her shoulder.

"One!" Kim said.

"You look like you could use one yourself."

Joyce put the bottle and a bowl of ice and two glasses on a tray. "Maybe Emtee would like a refill."

At that moment, Kim found the thought of a drink the most unappealing thing in the world. It was dreadful to think of Jane Corydon falling back into the habits she had broken herself of. What earthly good did it do to dull her senses with alcohol and make a fool of herself at the funeral of a man she apparently loved? Kim had an Irish distrust of drink, but it was a distrust that includes a lot of tolerance too. She might wish Jane Corydon had remained sober on this day of all days, yet she could not really condemn her. After all, she was an alcoholic and didn't that diminish her moral responsibility? It bothered her that Sister Mary Teresa was catering to Jane Corydon's sickness, but perhaps at the moment this was the beginning of a cure. But Kim could not herself have joined her in a drink for anything.

Nonetheless, Kim entered the study with a tray containing two glasses. Kim had seen Emtee Dempsey drink a dollop of sherry during the Christmas season, but nothing at any other time. Emtee indicated that Kim should put the tray on the desk. Jane Corydon was huddled in the leather chair across the desk from the little nun. With the tray before her, Sister Mary Teresa took over as if serving drinks to guests was one of her principal functions there on Walton Street. It occurred to Kim that this was the second time in a week they had served a guest drinks—first, Cheryl Pitman; now, Jane Corydon.

The ice clacked into the glasses. Glasses! Sister Mary

Teresa was preparing two drinks. She poured three ounces in one glass and three ounces in the other. She lifted off her chair in order to hand one of them to Jane Corydon.

"Here, my dear. This will brace you up."

Jane Corydon hesitated. "I've already had so much. I really don't think . . ."

"Nonsense. Another sip or two can't hurt you." Sister Mary Teresa picked up the other glass with what seemed a practiced hand. "Cheers."

And she put it to her lips and drank as if from real thirst. Kim was certain she would only feign to drink, but she was wrong. The level of the liquor was visibly down when the old nun returned the glass to the tray. From the opposite side of the desk, Jane Corydon watched her hostess drink. Did it surprise her? Perhaps she had already been sufficiently surprised to find herself in the same room with a religious in her centuries-old garb. Why should she find this study odd? Why should she find a bourbon-drinking nun odd? Kim's own mouth, she was sure, was wide open in amazement. And then Jane Corydon picked up her glass.

"Cheers," she said cheerlessly.

The ice cubes clattered against her teeth. Her eyes closed. She kept the glass to her lips and when she put it down Kim saw immediately that she had not drunk a drop. No doubt it was because her glass looked as she had expected Sister Mary Teresa's to look that she noticed it at all. Clearly, she had already had all she could handle and was not so drunk that she had thrown all caution to the winds.

"Isn't this your brand?" Emtee Dempsey asked, her tone one of maternal concern.

Jane Corydon professed not to understand the question. Emtee Dempsey showed her the label, Wild Turkey. Jane peered at it as if she couldn't see it. Perhaps she couldn't.

"What brand do you drink, dear?" Sister Mary Teresa asked sweetly.

"It doesn't matter." Jane Corydon spoke testily.

"I don't believe you are in the least bit drunk," Sister Mary Teresa said.

"That is hardly a fault," Jane Corydon said with her old primness.

"I doubt that you consumed any alcohol at all. What did you do, use it as a cologne? Why did you wish to appear intoxicated?"

Jane Corydon looked angrily at Kim, as if she were the explanation of the embarrassment she had caused herself. There seemed no doubt that her behavior at the funeral home, in the limousine on the way to and back from the cemetery, had been an act. And Kim had been a witness of it. Sister Mary Teresa turned to Kim.

"Would you leave us, please, Sister Kimberly. Dr. Corydon and I have something to talk about."

"The piece you are going to write on Birnam School?" Jane Corydon asked caustically, but she made no move to get up.

"I'm afraid so," said Emtee Dempsey.

"What did she mean by that?" Joyce asked a minute later in the kitchen. She was sipping on a drink she had made by pouring Jane Corydon's and Emtee Dempsey's glasses into a third.

"I don't know."

"How come she gave the guest more booze than she poured herself?"

"Joyce, she drank at least an ounce of bourbon. Neat."

"I don't believe it."

Kim left Joyce sipping skeptically on her scavenged bourbon and went upstairs to her room. When she lay back on her bed, her intention was simply to rest her eyes. The murmur of traffic from Walton Street, the melancholy but oddly soothing memories of that morning's funeral service, and tiredness too— she supposed the past few days had been wearing all conspired against her and she fell asleep.

She awoke and sat up, feeling guilty. She had not been asleep fifteen minutes. She hopped off the bed and went to where she had left her shoes, next to a chair across the room. The chair was by the window. Thus it was that she looked down and saw Jane Corydon step briskly into a cab.

Well, why not? Kim's sense of guilt stemmed from the feeling that, since she had brought Jane Corydon here to Walton Street, she was responsible for returning her to the Birnam School. Not that she wasn't relieved by the thought that she need not make the long westward drive and the equally long return. When she went downstairs, Joyce looked out of the kitchen. Her eyes seemed a little brighter than usual.

"Hi. I just checked and you were asleep. She wants you."

"Why didn't you wake me up?"

"I thought I had. I made a lot of noise getting the door shut."

Perhaps that had awakened her. "Dr. Corydon just left?"

"She didn't want a ride. I offered to take her." Joyce put a hand to her lips. Kim could smell the bourbon on her. Maybe Jane Corydon had too. What on earth was happening to them? First Sister Mary Teresa, now Joyce. Joyce was no surprise, perhaps. Kim knocked on the study door.

"I fell asleep."

"Dr. Corydon left a moment ago. She is a most interesting woman. But I already knew that from your reports. And Katherine's."

Reports? That seemed an exalted description of the conversations they had had after Kim's return from Birnam School.

"Why did you tell her she wasn't drunk?"

"She wasn't. She hadn't had a drop."

"But she was reeling."

"She told me herself, Sister. She had not had a thing to drink. I believe her."

"What made you suspect?"

"You had told me she was a reformed alcoholic. I reasoned that she would not make such a spectacle of backsliding."

"Why would she make a spectacle of herself at all?"

"Ah, the human heart," Emtee Dempsey sighed. "The human heart is baffling."

This was not a preface to any further explanation. Emtee Dempsey picked up a book. Kim was dismissed. She looked at the old nun, already absorbed in her reading.

Kim left the study. If Joyce had been a little noisy closing the door of her room, Kim was a trifle noisy shutting the study door. She marched down the hallway, breathing through her nose, fists clenched. She was as furious with herself as she was with Sister Mary Teresa, however. If she had kept her temper, she might have found out what else it was that Jane Corydon had not known, a not-knowing that might or might not be important. Oh, for heaven's sake. She went into the chapel, sat in a pew, and spent fifteen minutes trying to recapture some peace of mind. It helped to think of Miriam's Uncle Herbert, buried that day after the bland ceremony at the funeral home. Suddenly Kim found herself wondering if Jane Corydon's weeping had been any more genuine than her intoxication, and then she found the thought that the only one who had wept for Herbert was pretending to be, so sad that tears came to her own eyes. God bless him, she prayed. May his soul rest in peace. She remembered him as a gentle person whose concern had been that people should eat what he regarded as natural foods. It might seem quirky to her, but for all she knew there was much in it. She would be well advised to read all those books she had brought home for Sister Mary Teresa before she ventured to have an opinion on the matter. In any case, whether the foods he sold were as beneficial as he thought, he had thought they were, and surely there are worse ways to spend one's life than by providing healthful foods to others.

°   °   °

Two days later Cheryl Pitman died.

They received this news, Sister Mary Teresa and Kim, from Richard. He had come to Walton Street and when Kim came to the door and saw the expression on his face she opened the door quickly and asked no questions when he went by her without a word and on down the hallway to Sister Mary Teresa's study. He went right in and was already seated in the chair beside the desk when Kim followed him in. Sister Mary Teresa finished what she was writing, screwed her fountain pen together, made a neat little pile of her notes, and then pushed away from the desk slightly and looked at the two of them.

"Cheryl Pitman died twenty minutes ago," Richard announced in a monotone.

"God have mercy on her soul," Sister Mary Teresa said. "What happened?"

"She's been ailing since her brother's funeral." He could not keep a note of satisfaction from the remark. Since Kim's indictment, he had been taken off the Cheryl Pitman case and, though he had insisted he was more than happy to turn to more important matters, Kim knew how disappointed he must be by a reassignment that was an implied criticism. Yet now, what a blessing that he had not still been her guardian when she died.

"Ailing in what way?"

"That's unclear. Apparently she refused to see a doctor. Refused to admit she felt unwell. She said she could doctor herself."

"Oh?"

"She was a nut on natural remedies. It must have run in the family. She had an almost fanatical confidence in all that food stuff. Teas made from herbs, that kind of thing. It's funny, when you think of all the drives she took part in to raise money for various kinds of medical research, that she herself was content with . . ."

"Will there be an autopsy?"

"I don't know."

"There must be an autopsy," Sister Mary Teresa said. "Use my telephone. Now. I want you to insist that an autopsy be performed on the body of Cheryl Pitman."

"They will probably do one in any case."

"I cannot settle for probably. Richard, that woman was poisoned. It's clear as can be. Tell them that. There has to be an autopsy."

Still half bemused, Richard picked up the receiver of the phone she had pushed toward him. "Any particular poison?" he asked sardonically.

"I would guess pokeweed, but there are other possibilities."

Richard dialed while looking at Emtee Dempsey with a small incredulous smile. A minute later he was obviously happy the matter had been settled as it had. There would be an autopsy, as Sister Mary Teresa wished, but it had already been ordered as a matter of routine, and that exempted Richard from the need to insist something be done on the basis of an old woman's intuition.

"Intuition? Nonsense."

He was getting the best of that side of it too. His skepticism had not stopped him from suggesting that pokeweed be considered as probable cause of the nausea and vomiting that had plagued Mrs. Pitman for the past several days. Having said this, he put a hand over the receiver and whispered to Sister Mary Teresa. "Why should pokeweed be suspected?"

"Because of the herbal tea she drank. Have that analyzed too."

Richard passed the word along, hung up, and made what he should have realized would be the inflammatory reference to feminine intuition.

Sister Mary Teresa was as intuitive a person as one is likely to meet, but her theory of intuition separated it from women in particular and linked it to what she insisted on calling the other uses of reason.

"There are hunches, insights, intuitions. And they do

seem to come out of the blue. They don't. They are the fruit of half-conscious connections being made by the mind, swift inferences, seeing what a combination of things already known entails. You knew among innumerable other things A and B. When they are juxtaposed in your mind, you realize that C must be inferred from them. Take any intuition and you will find it is a species of deduction."

"But what is it that puts A and B together? What is it that selects them from all the other things I know?" Kim asked.

She snorted, "Explanations have to stop somewhere, child. You might as well ask why you know A and B in the first place."

So too now, having claimed with complete confidence that Cheryl Pitman had died of poisoning, most likely because of tea brewed from leaves containing pokeweed, she unscrewed her fountain pen, drew a fresh piece of paper before her, and was fully intent on getting back to her own work. To Richard's questions, and Kim's, she answered only that they already knew the premises from which she had inferred her "intuition" and she would not embarrass them by listing them.

"Embarrass me," Richard urged. "Embarrass the whole damned Chicago Police Department."

She was right. The elements of her answer, apart from lore she had gleaned from the books Kim had brought her on health foods, were the fact that Herbert's store specialized in the things it did, and that Cheryl Pitman had served Kim a vile tea when she visited her, a few sips of which had made her feel more than a little queazy. All the elements of the argument sustaining her surprising claim were, indeed, there for anyone to see. What was not there was any basis for the unshakable confidence with which she had drawn the conclusion.

"That is why the autopsy is important," she said.

"To verify your guess?"

She smiled. "No. To convince you it is not just a guess."

It was the irony of the occurrence that enabled Kim to overlook, at least to some degree, the smugness with which Sister Mary Teresa spoke. When Kim voiced this, however, she wanted to know in what sense Cheryl Pitman's death was ironic.

"Well, think of it. A week ago we hid her here, to protect her from an alleged threat on her life. Now she is dead, and if you are right, the victim of a freakish accident. She might have been cut down by bullets and she actually died because of the tea she drank."

"I did not say it was an accident."

Richard had risen from the chair when Kim began to muse aloud. Now he put his hands on the desk and looked down at Sister Mary Teresa.

"You mean someone poisoned her deliberately?"

Her mouth became a line for a moment. "That is not for me to say. All I say is that it was not an accident."

Accident or not, Cheryl Pitman was dead and Kim's thoughts turned immediately to poor little Miriam. How much more would the child be asked to bear? Already half an orphan, feeling abandoned by her mother at Birnam School, she had been shot at and injured, her Uncle Herbert, favorite of all her relatives, had been killed, and now, suddenly, her mother was dead. She had no one left but Amos Pitman, and Kim suspected that for Miriam this was equivalent to having no one left at all.

"I'm all right," she said.

What else could she say? But then, what else could Kim have asked than how she was? They sat in the living room where Kim had spoken with Cheryl Pitman. Miriam's eyes were red and Kim was almost relieved to see this sign that she had been weeping. Her voice, when she answered the stupid question, seemed to be squeezed from a constricted throat. Amos Pitman, who had appeared undecided whether to let Kim in, stood in the doorway for a moment, then turned and went away.

"I won't stay here with him," Miriam said with determination.

"You'll be going back to school."

"Summer's coming."

"Maybe you can go away to camp."

She nodded, looking out across the lake. It was a forlorn prospect, thinking of ways in which she could be away from this apartment, away from her stepfather, but after the cruel threat the man had made to Kim at Herbert's funeral, Kim could not bring herself to tell Miriam that she would learn to accept life with Amos Pitman. He had been her mother's husband, she herself bore his name as the result of adoption. Miriam might have been reading Kim's thoughts, for she said, in the same intense way she had said she would not live with Amos Pitman, "I will change my name back. I don't want to be called Miriam Pitman. It's not my name."

"Come stay with us at Walton Street."

She turned from the window and her eyes sparkled. "With the nuns?"

"Only one of us dresses like a nun, Miriam. And she is very old."

She put her hand on Kim's. "I want to go with you."

Her reaction diminished Kim's feeling of irresponsibility for having made the suggestion in the first place. Kim's excuse was that anything that might cheer up this tragic child seemed justified and the fact that she had spoken with such conviction of her unwillingness to face the prospect of a life with her stepfather made an invitation to come stay with them seem the most promising way to lift her spirits. Even as she said it, however, Kim recognized how unwise it was. Would Amos Pitman agree to Miriam's removal to a convent on Walton Street? The answer, to her immense surprise, was yes.

"Good. She can't stay here. Not now. I really don't know what to do with her. She's at an awkward age. Are there other children there?"

"She'll have companionship," Kim said.

He seemed bewildered himself by what had happened. "First Herbert. Now Cheryl." He shook his head. "I just can't believe it."

Who would look after Amos Pitman? He was now as alone as Miriam and there was no reason to think this would be much easier for him than it would be for her.

"And what of you?" Kim asked. "Is there someone to stay with you?"

He seemed surprised by her concern, even suspicious. "I'll be all right," he growled, exactly what Miriam had said before Kim had broken through her defenses.

He was mixing a drink when she went to help Miriam pack a few things. When they emerged, Kim was carrying Miriam's tote bag. Amos rose from his chair, setting down his drink, which tinkled like a leper's bell. Miriam hesitated, then crossed the room and held out her hand. He took it, his face distorted with uncustomary emotion. Then he pulled her to him and hugged her. His eyes squeezed shut and tears rolled down his face. It was all Kim could do not to cry herself when she saw Miriam's shoulders shake with sobbing.

Ten

In the wider world, during the next few days, things remained confused. A brother and a sister were dead, the one by gunshot, the other by poison. Orville and Mike were still at large. Even if they had been involved in Herbert's death—and it was Kim's fervent prayer that they had not been—it would have been difficult to implicate them in Cheryl's. One murder and one accident? That seemed perfectly plausible to Kim, but Emtee Dempsey vetoed it.

"Then come up with a better explanation."

"In time."

Kim held her tongue and left the study.

But if Emtee Dempsey was her usual enigmatic self, Miriam's presence in the house on Walton Street was an unmitigated delight. Joyce loved having her with her in the kitchen where the two of them made fudge and popcorn and tons of desserts. Miriam took a new interest in transforming the abstraction of a recipe into a savory reality and she could not have had a better tutor than Joyce. At other times, she sat in the leather chair in Sister Mary Teresa's study, a book on her lap, as absorbed in her reading as Emtee Dempsey was in her research. She came with the nuns to chapel, and if her manner was more wary there, she was clearly fascinated with the recitation of the Office. On the morning of the second day, Father Raush came to say Mass in their chapel, it being the anniversary of the death of the Blessed Abigail Keineswegs. As usual, at Sister Mary Teresa's insistence, he said the Mass in Latin.

"That is rare," Kim explained to Miriam at breakfast.

"Mass in the morning?" Emtee Dempsey asked. "Perhaps now. But it remains the best time of day. The hours that stretch ahead are put into perspective."

"I meant the Latin," Kim said, then wished she hadn't. She did not want to draw attention to one of Emtee Dempsey's pet peeves. The liturgy was all but always in the vernacular now, though English was optional, not mandatory. If the bishops were alarmed by what had happened, Kim did not know of it. But Miriam was not to hear Emtee Dempsey on this topic. Father Raush had gone back to the rectory immediately after saying Mass. The few times he had accepted the invitation to breakfast must have reminded him of grueling oral exams in the seminary. A conversation with Father Raush made Sister Mary Teresa shake her head.

"They are scraping the bottom of the barrel, there's no doubt of it. It wouldn't matter if the boy were a saint. Think of the Curé d'Ars."

"And Blessed Abigail," Joyce said perversely.

"The Curé d'Ars," Emtee repeated forcefully. "But, to be of mediocre spirituality as well as intelligence—well, that bodes no good."

"It was something like the synagogue," Miriam said.

"In what way?" Kim asked.

"I didn't understand a word."

"That is why Mass is usually said in English."

Surprisingly, Kim was allowed to have the last word on the subject. Sister Mary Teresa asked Miriam how often she went to the synagogue. It transpired that she had been there only once, the occasion sounded like a Bar Mitzvah, but Miriam didn't know.

"I want to be a nun," she said to Kim an hour later. She had come with Kim to her room and was reading in the basket chair while Kim pecked away at her typewriter. Kim nodded, as if she had not understood, and went on typing. It is something that crosses the mind of any Catholic girl at least once, usually to be rejected, but for Miriam it could only be a romantic fancy, on the level of the glow left from reading a novel by Rumer Godden.

"What do I do to become a nun?" she asked, her voice insistent.

Kim stopped typing. She smiled at Miriam, determined to strike the light note. "Well, first you have to get older. And it helps if you're a Catholic."

"I'll become a Catholic."

"Then you can become a nun."

"Should I talk to the priest about it?"

Kim took a cowardly way out. "First you might discuss it with Sister Mary Teresa. That's what I did."

To make sure they were beyond that topic of conversation, Kim got up and said she would show Miriam the room that had been shot to pieces the night her mother stayed in the house. Miriam was not very curious about it, even when Kim told her it was Emtee Dempsey's room. Of course the debris had long since been cleaned up and a temporary panel had been put in the door, so it was not the dramatic scene it had been that terrifying night. But standing there in the hall with Cheryl's daughter, Kim remembered the mother and her bravery and aplomb and it seemed incredible that she was dead. And Herbert dead as well. The fact that their deaths fitted into the tragic history of their family only made them sadder. What did it all mean? Kim was glad when Miriam went downstairs and left her alone with these somber thoughts.

The sequence of events that had begun with Richard's arrival on their doorstep with Cheryl Pitman made little sense. One thing happened after another, but it was difficult to see that one event happened because of another. Oh, no doubt Cheryl Pitman had been shot at in the house on Walton Street because Richard had brought her there, but that was hardly an illuminating fact. Kim sat at her desk and tried with such facts as she knew, supplemented by imagination, to make sense of what had happened.

At two in the morning, an hour or less before the bullets tore through the upstairs room, Cheryl Pitman had telephoned her husband. The phone call had at first appeared to be the explanation of the gunmen's knowledge of the room in which Cheryl was. If she had hired them to fake an attempt on her life, she could tell them where she was. But she had not called them, so how had they known? That they had known of the house in Michigan could be explained by imagining them watching the charade the following morning. Kim's attempt to deceive them by posing as Cheryl had not worked. Hanson had insisted, when Richard asked him, that Cheryl had made no phone calls from the house in Michigan. But she had hired Orville and Mike, if they could be believed. The trouble with this was that, as with the radio interview with Jane Corydon, a suggestion made by someone else became their story. Kim had brought up the explanation that they had been hired by Cheryl. The best she could derive from her memories of the conversation in the car was that they had not denied it, but their major concern was to be exonerated of any charge that they had attempted to injure a child. Why hadn't she continued her interrogation of that dipsy duo while they were staying in the house?

Because she found them comic. Kim simply could not

take them seriously. Herbert's description of them as immature men caught up in an imaginary game of cops and robbers seemed apt to Kim. But they had fled the house on Walton Street after she had spoken to them of Herbert, and Herbert had been shot with the convent Luger. Coincidence, circumstantial evidence, proof? Kim did not know. On the roof of the building from which they had shot at the house on Walton the imprint of their shoe soles bearing the legend "Oil Resistant" had been found. The shoeprints matched those found in the woods above the house at Union Pier as well as those in the stolen Michigan State Police car. But no such imprints had been found in Mother Nature's Dirty Diets. A negative fact. The disturbing fact was the Luger. Fingerprints? Certainly. Dozens of them. Emtee Dempsey's, Kim's, Cheryl Pitman's, others. But not Orville's or Mike's.

None of it made sense. *Cui bono?* What earthly advantage would Orville and Mike gain from Herbert's death? That they had their own quixotic code of honor was evidenced by their reaction to the suggestion that they might have taken part in an attack on Miriam. Would Herbert's derisive chortle constitute an unacceptable insult to their image of themselves? One sure beneficiary of the deaths of Herbert and Cheryl was Amos Pitman, but he was abject at what had happened. Adversity had brought him and Cheryl together again and his sense of loss, his general bewilderment at what had happened, seemed genuine to Kim. She forgave him the bitter words he had spoken to her at Herbert's funeral. Cheryl's funeral had not been lacking in tears, notably Amos Pitman's. He and Cheryl had been together in their boat anchored in Belmont Harbor when Herbert was shot, and she had clung to her husband when that news had come.

"She said we had to take Miriam out of Birnam School and keep her close to us. Herbert had been right about that, at least. It was wrong to put the child in a boarding school."

Kim nodded. So many good ideas would not be implemented now. Amos had not pretended inconsolable sorrow when Herbert died, but the death of Cheryl had turned him into a haggard, distracted man.

"That damned tea," he growled. "I never understood how she could drink it. But poison?" Amos looked at Kim, his expression demanding an explanation from her.

But if Amos was the beneficiary, it was impossible to make him Herbert's killer. He had been with Cheryl on the boat. And how could he have come into possession of their Luger?

The next day Joyce came upstairs to tell Kim she was wanted in the study and, on the way down, Kim wondered with a small smile if this summons had anything to do with Miriam's vocation to the religious life. But Miriam was not in the study.

"She's going to help me bake a cake," Joyce said, closing the door.

"News," Sister Mary Teresa said, waving Kim to a chair. "Cheryl Pitman did die of herbal poisoning. Pokeweed."

"You were right!"

"There is an oddity, however. The tea taken from the Pitman home by the police contained no trace of this substance."

"She kept the tea in a canister on the tea cart, but it was still in a paper bag."

"That is the tea they say they tested. No pokeweed."

"But that doesn't make any sense."

"Of course it makes sense. The tea she brewed was taken away and another bag substituted for it. Now, who would do that? The one responsible for her drinking the tea in the first place." The old nun smiled grimly. "So there is the proof that Cheryl Pitman's poisoning was not accidental."

"Sister, she got the tea from her brother who is now dead."

"The tea came from his store. I assume the accuracy of your identification of the bag that was in the canister on the tea cart. It bore the name of Herbert's store?"

"Yes. Mother Nature's Dirty Diets."

"The sack the police examined did not. It was a substitute. They will now devote their time and energy to discovering where the substitute sack came from." Emtee Dempsey spoke these words indulgently, as if the police would be cavorting harmlessly in conducting this search.

Kim said, "So whoever substituted that sack must be responsible for Cheryl's death?"

"*Might* be responsible."

"Amos Pitman?" Kim put the question timidly. The awful events of the past days had not made it easier for her to imagine one human being plotting the death of another. "*Cui bono?*"

Emtee Dempsey's brows lifted above the rims of her glasses, she sucked her lips between her teeth and shrugged expressively. All that added up to "perhaps" and, given the old nun's usual certainty, Kim was surprised. And relieved.

"Sister Kimberly, while the child is in the kitchen with Joyce, I want you to go up to her room and get the sack of tea in her tote bag."

"What! Are you serious?"

"It is there. I have seen it. Go get it, please."

What did Kim think of when she left the study, mounted the stairs, and went into Miriam's room? She kept her mind a blank, not wanting to connect this incredible errand with the reasoning she had just been engaged in with Sister Mary Teresa. The sack was in Miriam's tote bag, not at the top, but not squirreled away at the bottom either. It was just there, a sack of tea Kim was morally certain was the one from which Cheryl Pitman had brewed the cup that had made Kim feel poorly for several days. Kim actually held the sack away from her body, gripping the top of it with three fastidious fingers as she returned to the study: this was the tea that had killed Cheryl Pitman. Why had Miriam taken it away from the apartment? Why had she brought it here to Walton Street?

"Let's ask her," Sister Mary Teresa said.

"No!"

"Bring her in here."

"Sister, I can't."

Kim's mind fixed on the absurdity that she did not want Miriam to know she had gone into her room and taken something from her tote bag. She stared at Sister Mary Teresa.

"How did you know the tea was there?"

The old nun's brow nettled. "Your question is ambiguous. More accurately, amphibolous. Are you asking how I knew the tea must have been brought here by the girl, or are you asking the silly question as to how, while looking at the sack of tea, I managed to see it?"

"You knew it was there before I looked?"

"Of course."

Emtee Dempsey sat forward and put her hands flat on the desk. Her eyes sparkled with encouragement as if she expected Kim to repeat the inference that had brought her to the horrible conclusion it was Miriam who had substituted the one sack of tea for the other. But Kim had lost all interest in the game of deduction. They were speaking of a tragic little girl whose life had fallen completely apart. To conjecture that Miriam herself had helped pull her life apart made Kim sick at heart. She shook her head, rejecting the whole game.

Sister Mary Teresa began to frown, but her displeasure only increased Kim's desire to flee from the whole problem. What obligation did they have to pursue these suspicions when they promised only more tragedy? They should be doing something to soften the blows that had already fallen. Emtee Dempsey's objective curiosity, applied to the distant past, to history, was harmless enough, but turned on present events it struck Kim as inhuman, unchristian, worse than cruel.

When the doorbell rang, Kim responded as if it were a reprieve and scampered down the hall to answer it. On the doorstep stood Richard, flanked by Jane Corydon and Amos Pitman.

"Is she here?" Richard asked without preamble when Kim opened the door.

"Sister Mary Teresa?"

"Miriam," Jane Corydon said, fixing Kim with a cold eye. "We have come to fetch her."

"And I thought I could trust you," Amos Pitman said, hesitating a moment before following Jane Corydon down the hall to the study. Kim stared at him. Amos Pitman was a moral chameleon. She turned to Richard, who crossed his eyes in sympathy.

"The kid called Corydon," he said.

In the study, Amos Pitman was looking around at the book-lined walls, at the desk, at the leather chair. He sat. "I'd like a drink," he said.

Jane Corydon remained standing. "Miriam telephoned to say she intends to become a Catholic and then a nun."

Emtee Dempsey ignored her, speaking to Amos Pitman. "I understand the poison that caused your wife's death was pokeweed."

"Yes."

"Yet none was found in the tea from which presumably she had been drinking these past weeks."

Amos Pitman scowled. "I don't understand it."

"It seems quite simple to Sister Kimberly and me. We were just discussing it. Obviously someone replaced the tea your wife had been using with another sack." She opened her desk and brought out the tea Kim had taken from Miriam's tote bag. "This is the tea your wife had been brewing. This is the poison tea."

Richard, in the process of lighting a cigarette, choked. He looked angrily at Kim. "Is she kidding?"

"How did you get hold of that?" Amos Pitman's eyes were riveted to the sack of tea sitting only inches from him on the desk top. He reached out for it, his hand moving as it might have under water, but before he had it in his grasp, Richard swooped down on it.

"Kim," he barked, "did you take this from the Pitman apartment?"

"Aha." Jane Corydon lowered herself onto the arm of the leather chair and gave Kim a squinty-eyed triumphant look.

"The tea was brought here from the Pitman apartment," Emtee Dempsey said. "But not by Sister Kimberly."

"Miriam," Jane Corydon murmured, and then repeated it more loudly. "Miriam. Of course."

"What the hell do you mean?" Amos growled, looking up at her.

"She is suggesting that your stepdaughter is responsible for the poisoning of your wife," Sister Mary Teresa said calmly.

"Miriam?" Amos Pitman gave an imitation laugh. Then he leaned forward so he could see Richard. "She is a child of fourteen. Even if she were responsible for Cheryl's death, you couldn't bring charges against her."

"You may be right," Sister Mary Teresa said. "It would be a perfect crime."

"Is this the kid who wants to be a nun?" Richard asked.

"She already seems to have some of the qualifications," Jane Corydon said icily.

Richard demanded to know how Sister Mary Teresa had got hold of that tea and this brought Kim into it. She was asked to describe going upstairs and finding the tea in Miriam's tote bag.

"For all I know," Richard said, "this tea is no more harmful than the stuff we took from the apartment."

"It will have to be tested," Sister Mary Teresa agreed. "You will find pokeweed in it."

"The tote bag definitely belongs to the kid?"

Sister Mary Teresa spoke to Amos Pitman. "You remember the bag Miriam packed before coming here."

"Describe it." He seemed to have difficulty remembering the bag Kim described.

"Are you suggesting it is not your daughter's bag?" Sister Mary Teresa asked.

"I suppose it is. I just don't recognize it from the description."

"It is khaki with dark brown edging," Kim repeated.

"Maybe somebody exchanged tote bags as well as sacks of tea," Sister Mary Teresa said almost merrily.

"The tea came here in the tote bag," Richard said. "Okay. And the kid brought it here."

"But did she put it into the tote bag?" Emtee Dempsey said. "That is a separate question."

"Who else could have?"

"Sister Kimberly," Jane Corydon said with satisfaction, warming to the game.

"Or Amos Pitman," Emtee Dempsey said.

"I resent that."

"I put the tea in the tote bag."

It was Miriam. She had slipped quietly into the study unnoticed and apparently had been following the conversation. "I wanted to protect you," she said to Amos.

Amos Pitman sat forward in the leather chair and looked at Miriam with puzzled wonderment. The child had switched the tea in order to remove suspicion from him and he had difficulty knowing how to react. This meant she suspected him of murdering her mother but it also meant she had taken a risk to protect him from harm. He seemed to have difficulty believing anyone would wish him well without ulterior motive.

"My God, Miriam," he said, his voice breaking. "I would never have harmed your mother."

Jane Corydon, displaced from the arm of Amos Pitman's chair, watched with mixed feelings as Amos took Miriam into his arms. She might have been looking at a rival. She said, "Cheryl was her own worst enemy."

"Not while Herbert was alive," Amos said, still holding Miriam in his arms.

Jane turned to Kim. "You are the one who accused Cheryl of hiring men to shoot at her."

"Sister Kimberly was wrong," Emtee Dempsey said. "Miriam, would you run down to the basement and ask our guests to come up here?"

Richard was startled by this and he left the room on Miriam's heels. Emtee Dempsey rocked in her chair and the rest of them waited too. Kim recognized the voices of Orville and Mike long before they appeared in the doorway of the study. Orville pointed at Jane Corydon.

"That's her. She's the lady who hired us."

Mike chimed in. "We had nothing to do with the kid. She must have managed that by herself."

Jane Corydon was transfigured by this accusation. She turned toward the two gunmen, her face distorted with rage, and her first vocal reaction was a scream. Then she flew at them, to do what damage it would have been difficult to say. She never reached them. Amos Pitman ungallantly stuck out his leg and Jane Corydon pitched forward. It took Richard and Amos and Kim to subdue her. When she was in the leather chair, Richard stood behind her holding her shoulders while Kim and Amos held her arms to the arms of the chair. The scene had some of the aspects of an argument against capital punishment.

"She said she was Mrs. Pitman," Orville said.

"That is her ambition," Emtee Dempsey murmured.

"Did you hire these men to shoot at Cheryl?" Amos Pitman looked down at her as if she had just been discovered beneath a rock.

"But not hit her," Mike said. "Not hit her. The idea was to make it look good but not hurt anybody."

"Why, Jane? Why?"

Emtee Dempsey said. "Why Herbert, Dr. Corydon? Why did you kill him too?"

But Jane Corydon was looking in disbelief at Amos. "Why? How dare you ask me that. You know why."

Amos looked around at the others, his face a study in incredulity. This infuriated Jane Corydon.

"You wanted them dead. You wanted the money."

Amos let his mouth drop open. "You're crazy."

She began to struggle and Kim had difficulty holding onto her arm.

"You can't do this, Amos. You're as responsible as I am."

Kim had a vivid image of Amos Pitman sitting in Jane Corydon's office at the Birnam School. Had the two been lovers? Now he looked at her with amazed disgust while she gave him a venomous stare. Then she looked around, appealing to the others.

"We planned it together. Those two, Herbert, Cheryl."

Emtee Dempsey nodded as if she were still engaged in dispassionate analysis of events. "Sister kills brother, brother kills sister. Is that how it was supposed to look?"

"Yes!" Jane Corydon's eyes glinted and she nodded her head.

"Cheryl kill Herbert?" Amos once more laughed mirthlessly. "But, Jane, she was on the boat with me when Herbert was killed."

"The tea that poisoned Cheryl came from Herbert's store," Jane said, leaning toward Emtee Dempsey, as if the old nun was the one she must convince.

"A posthumous murder?"

Jane nodded eagerly.

"Did you take the tea from Herbert's store after you shot him?" Emtee Dempsey asked.

"Yes! And Amos exchanged it for her regular tea."

"The woman is deranged," Amos said, letting go of her arm.

Jane twisted free from Kim and lurched to her feet. She rushed at Amos, but not to harm him. She tried in vain to put her arms around him but he pushed her away, looking disgusted. Spurned, Jane Corydon became infuriated again and Richard pried her away from Amos, pulled her hands behind her back, and cuffed them. He looked at Amos for a moment, then turned to Orville and Mike.

"You two come with me."

"Take Amos too," Jane shrieked, but Richard steered her to the door.

Her wailing diminished as she went down the hall with Richard. Orville and Mike, having been assured by Sister Mary Teresa that they were in no real trouble, went docilely after. When the street door closed, silence fell.

"A woman scorned," Emtee Dempsey murmured, looking at Amos Pitman.

"I had no idea," Amos said, the sentence decrescendoing. A moment passed and then he added, "But I should have. I should have. My God, poor Cheryl."

He pressed his hands to the sides of his face and stared vacantly ahead. What did those unseeing eyes see? Kim remembered again Amos Pitman sitting in the headmistress's office at the Birnam School. Had he imagined he could enjoy a casual affair with a woman like Jane Corydon without stirring up a whirlwind? But whatever guilt he bore, it was not complicity in murder.

"They were right to call me," Emtee Dempsey said.

"Call you?" Kim asked. "Orville and Mike?"

But the old nun looked at Amos Pitman, who emerged from his anguished reverie and stared at her.

"When they saw your wife's photograph in the paper they realized she was not the Cheryl Pitman who had hired them. I convinced them they were safer here than anywhere else."

"Until everyone just dropped by for a visit?" Kim asked.

"Oh, Miriam called the gathering. Didn't you, dear? A phone call to Jane Corydon did the trick."

"Did she shoot Uncle Herbert?" Miriam asked.

Emtee Dempsey's brow clouded. "Take her home, Mr. Pitman. She has had enough excitement. We can leave the rest to the police."

Miriam said, "I'll get my tote bag."

Kim went to the front door with Amos Pitman and they waited there until Miriam came downstairs with her bag.

"I'll have them drop the charges against you," Amos Pitman said.

Kim looked at him in disbelief. The arrival of Miriam prevented her from saying something of which Blessed Abigail Keineswegs would have disapproved if she could have understood it. Miriam gave Kim a hug and went off with her stepfather.

Kim went back to the study and collapsed in the leather chair. Sister Mary Teresa looked at her over the rims of her glasses.

"Sister," Kim said, "for an awful time there I thought it was Miriam. I thought she had given her mother that tea. What a horrible thought."

"I thought the same thing for a time." She picked up her pen. "Thank God we were wrong."

For a minute the room was filled with the scratching of the old nun's pen.

"Why did Jane do it?"

Sister Mary Teresa pushed back from her desk and looked over Kim's head.

"Because she was in love with Amos Pitman. As she had been with Herbert. I assume that is how she would describe it." Emtee Dempsey sighed. "The things that are called love. Jane Corydon is a woman with enormous appetites. For wealth, for respectability. Katherine Senski was able to tell me much about her. Her drinking was a sign of that, I suppose. She met Herbert at a meeting of Alcoholics Anonymous. They had the same affliction. For a time they tried the same remedy, health foods. But it was doubtless Herbert's money that fascinated Jane

Corydon. And he kept throwing it away. Amos, on the other hand, shared her respect for money."

"She said they were in it together."

Emtee Dempsey made a sound that fluttered her lips. "Only in her imagination."

"But she'll tell the police the same story."

"I wouldn't worry about that."

Kim thought of Drew. "You're right. But will they ignore her for the right reason?"

"Amos Pitman is guilty of an ephemeral affair that Jane Corydon took infinitely more seriously than he did. She told me, sitting right where you are, that the reconciliation of Cheryl and Amos was a ruse. Her own conduct at Herbert's funeral was meant to rival what she considered Amos's tactic. Who would suspect her when she was so overcome by Herbert's death? Why, it had even driven her back to drink."

"You're convinced that Amos Pitman is innocent?"

"Innocent? No man is innocent, Sister Kimberly. But Amos Pitman will realize that he has much to regret."

"An affair with Jane Corydon?"

"That and being her unwitting accomplice."

"In what way?"

Emtee Dempsey sighed. "My dear girl, you were the one who discovered it."

Kim stared at the old nun. She hadn't the least idea what Emtee Dempsey was talking about.

"Tell me," Kim said, as furious with herself as with Sister Mary Teresa. How could she know what she did not know?

"The shots," Sister Mary Teresa said. "How did those men know Cheryl was in this house?"

Kim stood. Emtee Dempsey picked up her pen. It was to the accompaniment of its scratching that Kim left the study. She considered going to the kitchen and sneaking a smoke with Joyce. She thought of going up to her room and getting back to work as Sister Mary Teresa was doing. In the end, she went to the chapel where she knelt, put her face in her hands, and prayed for the repose of the souls of Cheryl and Herbert. But she was distracted by the thought of the phone call Cheryl had made from this house to Amos. And Amos, if Emtee Dempsey was right, had told Jane Corydon where Cheryl was spending the night. Had that provided an opportunity for the illicit lovers?

She sat back in the pew and tried to rid her mind of the awful consequences of a liaison that had apparently meant so little to Amos Pitman and so much to Jane Corydon. Emtee Dempsey was right. Amos might find regret as searing as guilt. She only hoped this would prompt him to make a better life for Miriam.

The chapel door opened behind her and the click of beads told her that it was Emtee Dempsey who had entered. The old nun sat down beside her, exhaling mightily as she did so.

"She reminded me of you, Sister."

"Who?"

"Miriam."

"In what way?"

"I remember when you first told me you wanted to become a nun."

Kim smiled. She had a vivid memory herself of that occasion. "You told me I wasn't the type."

"Did I?"

"You did."

"Well, considering the type I had in mind, I was right."

Kim turned to the old nun's mischievous smile. "Come, Sister, let's have a drink."

"A drink!" Kim cried.

"I asked Sister Joyce to make tea. Come."

And, as if she were taking up her vocation anew, Kim rose and followed Sister Mary Teresa out of the chapel.